Codename Prague,

An Unfinished

# PULP SCIENCE FICTION NOVEL

By

D. Harlan Wilson.

Book Two of the Scikungfi Trilogy.

## THE FIRST EDITION

Edited by Dr. Master Master Stanley Ashenbach Esquire.

**BOWIE:**
Printed by RAW DOG SCREAMING PRESS in *Maryland*,
and for STICK FIGURE INCORPORATED in *Pseudofolliculitis City*.

MMXI.

"*Dr. Identity* is a rollicking romp through a future so absurd, it can't help but feel real. D. Harlan Wilson shows us everything we know—but wish we didn't—about ourselves." **Robert Venditti**, author of *The Surrogates*

"Let's dispense with the usual predictable analogies ('Kafka/Cronenberg-on-laughing-gas'), redundancies ('Phillip K. Dick/William Gibson-on-acid'), or accurate-but-somewhat-obscure references ('the most intense and, in a certain sense, the most significant young prose writer since Mark Leyner and Ben Marcus...establishes Wilson as the Steve Katz of the post-everything generation...vies with Derek Pell's *The Little Red Book of Adobe LiveMotion* for being the funniest book of the new millennium'), and cut to the chase: D. Harlan Wilson's hilarious meta-pulp SF novel, *Dr. Identity*, is a funhouse mirror whose cartoonish distortions continually amaze and amuse—until one realizes that what we're seeing is a disturbingly accurate vision of ourselves. An instant avant-pop classic by a major new talent. Two surgically-enhanced, stainless-steel thumbs way, way up!" **Larry McCaffery**, editor of *Storming the Reality Studio* and *After Yesterday's Crash*

"This book's better'n the bushelful of Benzedrine-spiked donut holes with which Dr. Identity tries to bribe his students into civilized demeanor! Pomo cybertheory never tasted so good or made you fly this high!" ***American Book Review***

### BLANKETY BLANK: A MEMOIR OF VULGARIA

"With three offbeat story collections and the indescribably madcap *Dr. Identity* to his credit, Wilson has been duly anointed as speculative fiction's most unpredictable stylist. Here he flouts all novelistic conventions and propriety in recounting the misdeeds of a serial killer known only by a name written in blood on the walls of his victims' manicured homes—*Blankety Blank*. In the mid-twenty-first century, the American landscape has morphed from suburbia into "vulgaria," featuring neighborhoods replete with shopping malls and oversized McMansions. Quiggle Estates resident Rutger Van Trout just wants to enjoy his newly built silo in peace, without the added distractions of a nymphomaniac daughter, a werewolf-obsessed son, and a wife haunted by her own skeleton. Then Blankety Blank leaves his trail of blood across the vulgaria, and it's up to Rutger and Quiggle Estates' odd assortment of faux superheroes to save everyone. Wilson sprinkles his rapid-fire narrative with glib aphorisms, absurdist pseudo-historical tidbits, and outlandish digressions that leave a reader breathless. Although this isn't everyone's cup, iconoclasts will relish every word." ***Booklist***

"This is the fifth work of fiction from Wilson, a nearly unclassifiable Fabulist/ Satirist/Bizarro/Post-Postmodern/Speculative writer and literature professor whose titles include *The Kafka Effekt* and *Dr. Identity, or, Farewell to Plaquedemia*. Take an existential dive into the near-future's 'irreality' before the author sells out to Hollywood over a seemingly inevitable Gamehater movie." ***ForeWord Magazine***

"This comedy of menace, this spooky Kabuki, is never comfortable to inhabit but is as enjoyable as Krazy Kat just the same—the author indulges himself to the hilt and denies himself nothing." ***Rain Taxi***

"'Destroy time so that chaos may be ordered' was the instruction more than half a century ago of Mailer's Man Who Studied Yoga and D. Harlan Wilson has taken that advice seriously; here is a novel which implodes and conflates autobiography, biography, history, quasi-history, alternate history and Occam's Safety Razor in a fashion which I find utterly original and utterly discommoding. The exquisite tilt of this novel runs us all off the board and on; its originality is a weapon. Firing at that bullseye on time." **Barry N. Malzberg**, John Campbell Award-winning author of 70+ science fiction novels

"If you had a time machine and could secure the living brains of James Thurber and Andre Breton ripped untimely from their skulls, run them through a juicer, then mainline the blended liquid neurons, you might become a writer like D. Harlan Wilson. In fact, I know with certainty that this is how he actually got his start. As evidenced by his new 'Memoir of Vulgaria,' *Blankety Blank*, we are facing a writer who can evoke howls of pity and tears of laughter on the same page, and generally within the same sentence. In this 'multimedia' novel, suburban inanity and insanity are depicted in loving and intimate depth, resulting in a furiously animated canvas equal parts Bosch and Tex Avery. Imagine an episode of *The Simpsons* scripted by Robert Coover and Donald Barthelme, then directed by Michel Gondry, and you won't be far off the mark. If this be 'interstitial' fiction, then it's a case of the interstices expanding like a galaxy to overwhelm whatever bland shores once flanked them." **Paul Di Filippo**, author of *The Steampunk Trilogy*, *Ciphers* and *Cosmocopia*

## *PSEUDO-CITY*

"These intermeshed parables of madness and disjunction are funny the way that fever-dream of the naked fetuses squirming silently on a sidewalk you had last night is funny—when you think back on it sometime around noon today. At the brain stem of this impressive, relentless, heterologic schizopolis crouches a reptilian complex that would make Kafka, Burroughs, Bataille, and Leyner grin in recognition and admiration." **Lance Olsen**, author of *Nietzsche's Kisses* and *Tonguing the Zeitgeist*

"Only D. Harlan Wilson could make a stick figure more entertaining than most human beings. I haven't read a Wilson story I didn't go bug-eyes over. He delivers the surreal like no other writer working today, and his latest book is the master surrealist at his best. *Pseudo-City* is an ingenious subversion—the sort of book that has the power to change your entire perception of the everyday world. You'll be laughing when you read it, wondering if you've just tipped over into madness. But you won't care because it feels so damned good. Enjoy the vertigo, folks!" **Michael Arnzen**, Bram Stoker Award-winning author of *100 Jolts* and *Grave Markings*

Published by Raw Dog Screaming Press
Bowie, MD

First Edition

Cover image: Brett Weldele
Book design: Jennifer Barnes

Printed in the United States of America

ISBN 978-1-935738-05-3

Library of Congress Control Number: 2010934339

www.RawDogScreaming.com

# 代号布拉格

## QUOTES

Galveston, oh Galveston,
I still hear your sea waves crashing
while I watch the cannons flashing.
I clean my gun and dream of Galveston.

—Glenn Campbell, "Galveston"

Yellow man in Timbuktu—
color for both me and you.
Kung fu fighting, dancing queen,
tribal spaceman and all that's in between.

—The Spice Girls, "Spice Up Your Life"

It's a great day for genocide. (What's that?)
That's the day all the niggaz died.
They killed JFK in '63.
So what the fuck you think they'll do to me?

—Ice Cube, "When Will They Shoot?"

## DEDICATION

For all the aborted and unrealized acronyms.

# TABLE OF CONTENTS

Introduction.................................................................... 17

**00** Slomo Scikungfi .................................................. 21

**01** Slaughterhouse-Five ........................................ 29

**02** The Case of the Errant Bottle of Carbonated Olive Oil ........................ 35

**03** Interview with a MAP Man................................ 45

**04** The Scorcese Boys ........................................... 53

**05** Cirque de Socius.............................................. 59

**06** The Count of Vincent Prague ........................ 67

**07** Eleven Mad Scientists & Fifty-Five Monsters........................ 69

**08** Houses of If ...................................................... 77

**09** Untitled Teufelsdröchk Rejektion Letter ................ 85

**10** Tranzatlanticism ............................................. 89

**11** Araby (Re)vis[it]ed ........................................ 97

**12** Statue of Libashout ........................................ 105

**13** Two Mad Assistants & Two Assistant Monsters....................... 107

**14** The Hotel Prague ............................................ 109

**15** The Prague Delova.......................................... 115

**16** Pragensia St Cagney ...................................... 121

**429** AR .................................................................. 125

**17** The Sans Merci vs. Macavity the Master Criminal................... 127

**20** In Outer Space, a Ceramic Mannequin without Arms & a Cracked Foot...... 135

**29** *Passagenwerk* ............................................... 137

**32** Houses of If II: The Sequel............................. 151

**33** Elevator Pitch ................................................. 153

**42** Houses of If III: The Interquel (a.k.a. Revenge of the Scikungfighter).......... 155

**448** *Daikaiju* Blues at the Bruce Lee Funpark.................... 157

**48** There Is a Hole Here Where Something Else Used to Be ............... 171

**51** The Resistance of Memory .............................. 173

**56** Amerikan Hemorrhage Dictionary of Scikungfi................. 177

**1007** Short Fable ................................................... 179

**1008** Long Fable .................................................... 181

**1111** Untitled Prague Rejektion Letter.................... 183

**1517** The Death of Doktor Hermann Teufelsdröchk ................. 185

**-66.799** The Nowhere Incident ................................ 189

**#** Codename Prague ............................................ 191

## DEFINITIONS

大怪獣 *daikaiju* (dah•gwhy•zhü) Giant cinematic monster(s). Also denotes the genre of films featuring giant monsters. Common sobriquet: "The Tall Angry One Who Induces Hot Ubiquitous Gore." Distinguished by alienation, loneliness and anger, even in large numbers.

**ekphrasis (ek•frə•səs)** A graphic, ultraviolent depiction of a visual work of reality.

*—The Amerikan Hemorrhage Dictionary of Scikungfi*

# DRAMATIS PERSONÆ

*With the names of the original actors and reality studios in alphabetical order.*
*(Note: Incl. only players with vital speaking roles and guild cards.)*

## MEN & ALIENS

Administrator Wichita
Araby Manager 1
Araby Manager 2
Araby Manager 3
Araby Manager 4
Araby Manager 5
Araby Manager 6
Araby Manager 7
Beauty / Ugly
Bystander 1
Bystander 2
Bystander 3
Commodore Ronald Rabelais
Doktor Hans Reinhart
Doktor Hermann Teufelsdröckh
Doktor Hermann Teufelsdröckh's Father
Doktor Ray B Flechsig
Flight Attendant (Amerika Slingpad)
Flight Attendant (Prague Slingpad)
Gentleman 1
Gentleman 2
Gentleman 3
Henri Prague
Man in a Letter P Costume
Nobody 1
Nobody 2
Nobody 3
Percussionist
Production Manager of *Cats*
Rardion (a.k.a. "Mike") the Bazaar Greeter
Salvador Dali
SAMSA 066
SAMSA 067
Stagehand
Truth / Untruth
Usher
Vincent Prague a.k.a. Vincent "Codename" Prague
Vincent Prague a.k.a. Vincent "Codename" Prague's Father

## MEN DRESSED AS WOMEN

Delilah Jive
Femme Fatale 1 (Mädchen "The Prague" Prague)
Femme Fatale 2 (Sindie Switch )


## HYBRIDS, ANDROIDS & MONSTERS

Armand Dorleac
Beauty / Ugly Monster
Bouncer
Bustopher Jones
Donald Pleasence *Wütendeswissenschaftlermunster* 1
Donald Pleasence / Alien *Wütendeswissenschaftlermunster* 2
Hitler / Keats Hybrid + *Daikaiju* Monster a.k.a. The Sans Merci
James Cagney
James Joyce
(Macaulay) Culkin
Macavity Cat
Man with a Goat Head
Monster Peddler
Riddler Jim Carrey perf. CSI David Caruso
Scorcese Boy 1 (Niky Santoro)
Scorcese Boy 2 (Bill the Butcher)
Scorcese Boy 3 (Max Cady)
Scorcese Boy 4 (Tommy DeVito)
Scorcese Boy 5 (Francis Costello)
Scorcese Boy 6 (Travis Bickle)
Solomon Grundy Bruce Lee
Truth / Untruth Monster
Zero Punctuation Expobot


## UNCLASSIFIABLE PLAYERS

The Nowhere Man


## SETTINGS

Château d'If, Brazil
City City, USAmerika
Hong Kong, China
Prague, Former Czech Republik

# Introduction
## by Steve Aylett

Certain memories become sacred. In D. Harlan Wilson's case, it was the time he tripped and fell into an ancient liturgical drama, swearing point-blank into the face of a bishop long dead. He then wounded nineteen people while running amok in that antique realm, as the metal-clawed creature later known to history as "Spring-Heeled Jack." Thus he knew paradise and lost it. Wilson is now as helpless before the dictates of his moods and whims as he was before the violent wormhole calamities of childhood. But that is unimportant. What matters is that he exists and that he was made aware of the fact before we were. Everyone has experienced the dismal waste of time that can be inflicted by those who wish us to know them before they know themselves. This is a crime for which Kermit the Frog has yet to be punished, unless you count the fact that he can't stop moving his arms.

It is not unusual for the memory to condense into a single mythical moment the contingencies and practicalities of artistic inspiration. Wilson claims he decided to write his barbaric and erudite Scikungfi Trilogy while trying to inflate some sort of pool toy, an exercise at which he repeatedly failed until collapsing into tears, a pathetic sight for one and all. That crude vinyl icon of a camel, dented and lopsided, hung from his lap like every failure in his life. Wilson's life can indeed be divided into two parts: before and after this sacramental defeat. It was a bankruptcy localized enough to be effective—effortlessly checkmated by a novelty plaything, what could he do but overcompensate, creating a mental yakuza in which he could demand massive respect? The accident riveted him to a public downfall like a voodoo chicken to the door of a grateful Catholic priest, who cooks the mascot for his happy family. The scornful gaze of Wilson's friends as he let the flaccid toy slip from his slack hands transformed him into a constituted nature. He dreamed of a world in which his powers—those of the mind—are respected. Such a world does not as yet exist, but he can imagine one in the very mind that desires respect—thus creating a vortical involution resembling his inefficiently pursed lips during that initial washout of an afternoon.

We can surmise that this decision will be of capital importance—to say, in defiance of all, I Will Not Merely Be A Beaky Buffoon For You Bastards. Rather than a journey to the end of his misfortune, he invents a way out via a character who can make a blow to the face last a week. An altar of asphalt and sugar bulges from Wilson's fireplace, embedded with femurs and vintage Vickers ammunition belts. He can immerse his books in concrete detail—coincidentally a fate the mob have had in mind for him since he crashed one of their meetings in a monster truck and leaned out to explain that the universe is "not motivated by obligation—where's your Omerta now?" Such mad confidence within despair will bear grim fruit. It spies on its own inner life and discovers electric mischief elves pounding up eternal-repetition exit ramps aglow. To the right-thinking man these denote only psychosis, yet these are what Wilson offers to others in the guise of "supporting players." Sure of possessing the ground spice created from exploding truth at supercompressed angles (actually the corner of someone else's barn) and concerned only with being seen in this undertaking, he expects to be tolerated. If he looks at himself in this mirror, he sees the accelerated colors of his magically-clad transparencies, at vertices to each other and tagged with self-triggering name-clues that should be obvious to you, reader. We have seen that, as a result of his multidimensional misfortunes as a child and his public inadequacy as an adult, he has dreamed of raising himself above men. Despite the daily battering of a thousand bitter truths, this dream has never left him. Society, too, defends itself against the barrage of facts present and latent in the universe, against the numinous and the precise, by means of custom—that is, by a body of consensual observances. Inversely, infraction of the customary rules invests the offender with a sacred aura because it confers upon him the power to unloose truthful powers—though whether he chooses to use his oblique position for this purpose is another matter. In *Tarka the Otter* we find that Henry Williamson has used the outcast position merely to talk about an otter and "his joyful water life," deftly skirting the explosive issues of scorching sedition and profanely exotic rebellion almost any other writer would have explored.

Not all prose springs from the intention to communicate—whether it be meaning, disease, magnified truculence, secrets manufactured specifically to be revealed, a market mysticism of betrayal, centuries-interrupted doom plots at last resumed, the innocent back of a monster, sham delights, applicable death-blows or the custom joinery of Trojan-viral prayer. Those who have drugged furniture, diabolified dialogue and sacrificed storyline in a desperate attempt to stray from current literature's cheap, worn paradox and pre-explained heroes deliver a merciless cure, a dimly-lit liberation that leaves the reader with the final responsibility to walk away from this trash-catharsis and start using his or her brain, if only in miniature. Beyond this, the frenzied and exacting works of quantum pointillists such as Jeff Lint, Violaine and Eddie Gamete leave their stains at the high-tide mark of psychodimensional exploration where no one thinks to look.

Wilson's propulsion from hydraulic misfortune to a rambunctious form of expression, his spirited attempts to wear the reader's face for a hat, and the final, very public siege and arrest which exposed both him and his doll-filled basement to the American media, are now well-known. There is a thriving market—from which he does not profit—in t-shirts bearing the notorious mug-shot in which he is seen to have twelve eyes, all of them closed. The trial itself is better known for the sudden exhibition of Wilson's "energy snake" than any meaningful discourse on literature. My hopes for an awakened interest in hypervortexal fiction came to an end with that childish display and the subsequent descent into flailing drop-kicks and hollering ushers. Since the debacle Wilson has been publicly defined as a snorting disaster-pig and his technical and creative gifts have been relegated to the realm of myth (or what Marshall Hurk has called "the secret place of honor"). It is hard to gauge how it has affected his personality, just as it is difficult to measure to the millimeter the distance traveled by a swarm.

Certainly he could never sustain the half-mad state of nervous excitement he displayed in the courtroom. In recent photographs he stares as if stunned by a blowfish.

Although Wilson will no doubt remain an enigma to some, as one who has made a tremendous contribution to the immense story of human violence, his work is sure to generate frantic evasion and nervous disdain amid the follower-filled timidity of modern scholarship, and a wide readership among the groundlessly triumphant, the conspicuously fanged and the seeking.

The public image of The Author—ramrod straight, unsurprised and studded with snails that make a popping sound when removed—has given way to the general impression of a force intent on using as many words as possible to say nothing we don't already know. It's a choice between those who were once alive or those who are now dead. Faced with an industry impermeable to talent, real creators will turn in another direction and aim at a heightened target, a unique emblem all bedecked with resinous blossoms and chained fruit. It may feel like a mixture of a stingray, a valentine and a nasty bump on the noggin. An abyss of treasure, detail-rich and explorable at every scale. For myself, I would ask a favor of everyone reading this introduction. If you're going to write, write something interesting and original, or get the fuck out of the way.

—London 2009

# OO
## Slowmo Scikungfi

After he assassinated the Nowhere Man, the Ministry of Applied Pressure told Vincent Prague to go to hell. Subsequently he was appointed to the position of Anvil-in-Chief, the catbird's seat of special agents. "If he can off Nowhere, he can do anything," was the Ministry's belated logic.

Two MAP agents snuck into Prague's conapt to deliver the news. They wore standard MAP attire: Casablanca fedoras, photoelectric razorshades, sharply defined beetledream suits. They raided the refrigerator, set up a system of wiretaps, and tiptoed into the bedroom. Prague slept naked atop the covers in a fetal curl. His lips quivered like divining rods.

"Wake up, Mr Prague," barked an agent, chewing a piece of ginger broccoli. The other agent turned on the lights.

An alarm went off.

The alarm triggered an antigravity shockwave that lifted all bodies and objects not nailed to the floor into the air. Vincent Prague remained asleep. He didn't wake up until an agent hurled a throwing star at the alarm, silencing it in a plume of blue sparks. The star had been rigged to disavow the room's cavoritic conversion.

"Who's there?" said Prague. He bumped into the ceiling. "The lights are on."

The agents traded confused expressions. One droned, "Put us down, sir."

Prague smiled a crooked smile. "The lights are on," he reiterated.

Confusion slipped into consternation. The agents had never met Vincent Prague. But they knew of him. Skinny fella. Tall fella. Good killer. Shitty attitude.

The agents' names—SAMSA 066 and SAMSA 067—scrolled around the belts of their fedoras in a pulsing LED libretto. Hanging comfortably in the air, SAMSA 067 clenched his fists. His knuckles cracked like popcorn. SAMSA 066 grinned and rearranged the nub of his tie. "We're trained for combat in non-gravitational spatialities," he said. "Hard or easy, Mr Prague. Either way you're coming with us."

Prague scratched an armpit. "Non-gravitational spatialities? What're you, my grandmother?"

"Hard, then," said SAMSA 067. SAMSA 066 flexed his jaw. "Have it your way."

Lack of gravity rendered the consequent scikungfi fight a decidedly slow motion affair. The agents converged on Prague, swinging their arms in wide circles and using floating pieces of furniture, books, bongs, televisions for leverage. They moved forward like unmanned zeppelins. Arms neatly folded behind his back, Prague waited for them to get closer. At one point he snatched a graphic novel that floated by and thumbed through it.

Half a minute later the agents were almost within reach. Antennae and fossorial legs sprouted from their beetledream suits as they prepared to strike. They could kill him if they saw fit. They could even cut him into pieces. The MAP would reanimate and stitch his body back together. Prague had already been reanimated twice, once after being gunned down by a rival assassin, the second time during a friendly water balloon fight that went sour and turned into a hydrochloric acid war. Briefly he adopted a third-time's-a-charm sensibility. But reanimation was a messy, tiresome business; he couldn't be bothered with it. And he hadn't scikungfi fought in antigravity for years.

"I'll give you dipshits first crack," Prague said. "Be nice now. I'm still half asleep."

SAMSA 066 attacked with a snap kick. Prague didn't move, didn't even flinch—he let the kick land on his jaw. His head ricocheted off his shoulder and bounced back into place as the agent leisurely somersaulted by...

SAMSA 067 lashed out with an antenna that crackled and fizzed with electricity. The antenna sliced through Prague's flesh like butter, claiming his right ear lobe. Toiletbowl blue globules of Victory brand gin floated out of the wound.

Prague let it bleed.

"This is no way to treat a man in his birthday suit," he said. Gripping the blade of a ceiling fan for support, he swung a knee into SAMSA 067's groin. The agent squealed and slapped him across the face with an insect leg. Prague grabbed his balls and squeezed...The agent writhed, growled. They were eye to eye and his breath smelled of stale gasoline. Prague winced, released his balls and delivered two sharp fists to SAMSA 067's chest. He pinwheeled away just as SAMSA 066, who had gained momentum by springing off a wall, returned for a second assault.

The agent pulled a Weird Science gat. Prague had seen the model before: a shiny steampunk raygun in quasinautical motif with radiator fins and Babbage bulbs. Brain-melting hardware. Possibly a zombification tube. Either effekt suited him. As a teenager, he and his friends spent most of their time shooting themselves in the heads with rayguns. Better than sex. Better than pharmaceuticals. Almost better than virtuality. It took some getting used to, and a few friends permanently lobotomized themselves—Timmy McFarlin accidentally suicided, morphing his thinkball into a mushroom omelet. But generally the boys acclimatized to the neuroviolence. Prague took a special liking to it. He couldn't function unless he shot himself in the face with an aether oscillator for no less than ten seconds eight times a day. A few stints in rehab cleaned him up. He wished he could go back, though. He'd do it all over, just the same.

"Put your hands up, Mr Prague," said SAMSA 066.

"And if he doesn't answer?" said Prague.

"Let me see those hands, Thin Man," said the SAMSA.

"And if he still doesn't answer?" said Prague.

SAMSA 066 frowned philosophically. "I simply say...♪Baby, oh baby, my sweet baby, you're the one...♪"

Prague shook his head. "You silly asshole. Nobody puts Baby in a corner."

When the agent floated within range, Prague snatched the gun from his hand and nailed him on the forehead with the handle, shattering the LED screen of his fedora. He hurled the gun at SAMSA 067, who languished in a ceiling corner. The weapon drifted end over end and innocuously bounced off of the agent's hip.

As the agents struggled to rally, Prague took a time out to dress his wound. He swam down to the floor, pulled himself across shag carpet to a mini-fridge and removed a spare ear, custom-made for his physiology and DNA. He kept spares of most of his external body parts in the mini-fridge. He had three more ears, two extra noses, a chin, fingers and toes, eight sets of genitals (male and female), several eyeballs, several eyebrows, and a handful of mouths. All costly items, but nothing that couldn't be negotiated by massive financial debt, ensuring that countless members of the postcapitalist universe were as good as Mr Potato Head.

In order to replace the sliced off lobe, Prague needed to hack off the remainder of his ear. He used a monofilament saw that cauterized the wound it made as the damaged ear curled off of his head like the skin of a pear. Teeth clenched, he held the replacement ear to the wound and waited for its minute, hungry roots to sink in...His brain became a worm farm. A torrent of flashbacks besieged him. A life passed before his eyes... He saw himself spit from the bearded mouth of a womb like a pinch of tobacco...He saw himself devouring a birthday cake and tearing through a jungle of crepe paper...He saw times tables, Sea Monkeys®, superscreens, monoliths...Yul Brynner in *Westworld*. His face fell off to reveal...legion of soldiers with goat heads goosestepping down the streets of City City...There was a deep, unrecognized, unprecedented kiss. He could hear the kiss over the screaming of the worms...Subtitles formed beneath his feet. He wore a pharaohic graduation gown that metamorphosed into a seersucker lounge suit. The subtitles read: *Sha na na na, sha na na na na*...Prague sitting behind a desk. Prague observing a pencil. Prague clocking out. Prague sailor-diving into a lake of fire...robotic drill sergeants and starship troopers and Continental Ops...mosaic of warzones from different time periods. Scikungfi fighting from here to eternity...image of a dimly lit red lamp in a motel room. In the bathroom, a toilet flushed...vista of Nowhere. The man fell to his knees and burned like a scarecrow...

...the wound sealed over. Prague shook his head. Mnemonic vestiges broke apart, dissolved...He touched the ear. Tugged on it. No pain. No problem.

He stood.

Not only had the agents regained their composure, they were right behind him, reaching out for him. He could smell their oiled extremities.

Prague clapped his hands. The room flooded with gravitons.

Everything fell. The agents slammed into the floor like sacks of clay. SAMSA 067 was incapacitated by a television that landed on his head, cracking his skull. Heavy and dense as a boat anchor, the television was an old, refurbished '59 Silvertone Suburbanite. SAMSA 066 dizzily got to his feet. Kinked legs folded back into his suit. He took off his razorshades. He looked at his partner. He looked at Prague.

"One of these days I'll have to get a futuristic TV," said the Anvil-in-Chief. "Thing is, I only buy vintage."

SAMSA 066 blinked. "What happened?"

"It's the clapper. New twist on an old hat. But you ain't seen nut'n honey." Prague clapped his hands again, twice.

Realtime slipped into fasttime.

SAMSA 066 had limited experience in fasttime. To become an agent of the Ministry of Applied Pressure, he endured countless hours of requisite irrealtime training. But that was long ago, and he had never been in a fasttime fight on the job. He resembled a crash test dummy in a windstorm as Prague rained blows all over his body and the agent twitched groaned flailed and Prague attacked with an arsenal of martial arts moves karate tae kwon do kung fu jeet kune do judo aikido escrima hapkido muay thai t'ai chi ninjutsu all the major styles were represented including a few esoteric forms vale tudo capoeira krav maga dim mak pankration mu tau shootboxing all reinforced by a staunch wuxia ethos and he concluded with a Mr Miyagi sandblaster followed closely by a token Bruceploitation punch and finally a *daikaiju* blaster which hit SAMSA 066 like a big rig in maximum overdrive and the agent's ribcage fractured into hundreds of pieces the blow was so devastating and hideous and his body hit the floor and spun around and around and around and the agent squeaked something and then everything was still and silent and peaceful for a second or two.

A vidphone rang like an Uzi.

Prague clapped fasttime back into realtime. The ring slowed down. He pushed an audio button on the vidphone console. "This is a recording," he said, and hung up.

He surveyed the bedroom. What a mess. He was a neat freak with the vaguest touch of OCD and the *mise en scène* didn't sit well with him. Leave it to the government to exacerbate a citizen's god-given disorder.

"Underwear," he intoned. A pair of pinstripe boxer briefs tumbled out of a closet. They scuttled across the floor and up his legs and snarled into place.

He took SAMSA 066 by the arm and dragged him into a corner, trying not to get the toothpaste that the agent bled on his skin. SAMSA 067 bled electric ants. In the universe of fashionized ultraviolence and reanimation, virtually everybody had swapped their blood for something chic, or at least something that wasn't blood, which is to say, something that didn't look like blood but contained all of its essential ingredients (with the addition of sundry varieties of Hamburger Helper). Many citizens had surrogated their organs with inanimate objects, too, ranging from fruits and vegetables to sand and stuffed animals. Prague wondered how SAMSA 067 afforded the ants. Posh dialysis by anyone's standards. A Victory gin martini was the best Prague could do on his embarrassing income. One day, in his own private Idaho, he hoped to upgrade to Hammer blood, the voguest artificial brand on the market. Or at least a martini mixed from Steinhäger.

SAMSA 066's mouth was a serrated hole. "You killed my partner," the hole wheezed. "You killed me."

Prague clicked his tongue. "They can rebuild you. They have the technology."

SAMSA 066 swore. And died.

The vidphone rang again. Prague watched it ring.

Fifteen rings later he answered the call.

Rabelais. Commodore Ronald Rabelais. General Assistant Managerial Choreographer of Mortal Affairs for the Ministry of Applied Pressure's

Department of Anthropologism. He fizzled into view in the guise of Marvin the Martian. Prague's vidphone had a catatonic converter that portrayed callers as Looney Toon characters on its screen. What Looney Toon character it was depended on one's physiognomy, physique and personality, all of which were gauged by the teleanalytic finesse of the vidphone's Transparent Eyeball. Callers were cartoonized based on which character they looked and acted like the most. With Rabelais it was a no-brainer. Except for being Caucazoid, he sort of resembled Marvin the Martian in real life with his thin limbs, big eyes, and round head. He was a small man, too—a hairdo's breadth away from Lilliputian. And as long as Prague had known him, he had, like the Martian, always demonstrated a cosmic death drive and a steel-toothed love of thanatopsis.

"Ah, Vincent," chirped Rabelais in a muffled, kazoolike voice. "There you are." He stood center-screen in token broomhead hat, kilt and sneakers. Apropos his skin was jet black.

"Here I am," uttered Prague.

"Well then. I trust you're on your way out the door? They're waiting for you at the slaughterhouse. I hope my boys haven't given you any trouble. Boys will be boys."

Prague looked over his shoulder at the ramparts of the SAMSAs. "I don't think your boys'll be home for dinner, Pops."

Cdre Rabelais nodded gravely. "I see." He lifted his chin. He scratched his chin. He started to pace back and forth across the north pole of the little red planet beneath him. "Reanimation is a costly affair. Reanimation is a costly affair." He kept saying it.

Prague sighed. "Look. Spit it out. I'm out of one-liners and it's time for breakfast. Eggs and bacon. No toast." Was the Commodore really sore because he put two measly functionaries out of their misery, if only temporarily? Or was it the usual exhibition of short man's syndrome? Prague couldn't tell. He could never tell what was eating Rabelais. But he knew better than to assume a short man living under technopatriarchal constraints wasn't bitter to the core.

"It's OK, it's OK," said the Commodore dryly. "I promise not to cry."

"I cry. I cry all the time. Have you seen my wardrobe? It's a burlap factory in there."

Cdre Rabelais stopped pacing, faced Prague, and forced a plastic grin. "At any rate, you know what this is about, yes? The MAP needs you. You're back in. I need your magic, as the Bearded Walrus says. No questions asked. Figure it out."

"What if I don't want back in? I killed Nowhere. What did I get in return? Tupperware. Walking papers. A dick in the ass."

Cdre Rabelais ripped off his hat and hurled it into space. His black, bald head disappeared into the onyx backdrop. "Get the fuck in here!" he exclaimed. "Do it! Do it! Do it! Do it!" Rabelais paused, collected himself. And in a soft voice: "Since I have you on the line, Vinnie, we might as well talk about a name. A codename, to be precise. New case, new name. Any ideas? There's a team of ghostwriters brainstorming as we speak. We can't have you walking around like a plebe with your real name. You need an artificial name."

Prague stuck out his lips. "I've got an artificial name. Call me...Prague. Call me Codename Prague. My real name will be the mark of my artificiality—the ultimate disguise."

Fighting off another outburst, Rabelais closed round white eyes. "Right. Hm. I'm not sure if that sobriquet does the trick. Identity is a delicate matter. Let's not rush the matter. Let's—"

Marvin the Martian disappeared. THE END, read the grey screen of the vidphone.

# 01
## Slaughterhouse-Five

The Slaughterhouse District ruptured the sleek geometry of City City in a jagged bulge of steeples, chimneys, ducts, pipelines, escalators, elevators, fire escapes and smokestacks. The buildings were black, sharp, latticed by tiny blue windows. Gold-rimmed gondolas whizzed across the metallic grey sky on thin tracks of wire. Periodically the shadow of a man in a bird suit passed through the moon, a great jaundiced globe that hung above the night like a tumor.

Taste of copper, fluoride, soot...

...the mouth of a docking cove in Slaughterhouse-Five swallowed a quiet gondola.

The doors scraped open. A flock of smoldering fedoras poured out and disappeared into a long row of antique elevators...

...elevator attendants in colorful, brimless hats told jokes about ballerinas— the one about the emaciated ballerina, the one about the buck-toothed ballerina, the one about the arthritic ballerina, the one about the ballerina who had a lisp, the one about the ballerina who overdosed on anaphora...

Laff tracks flared. Cigarette embers pulsed.

Floors dinged.

...From one end of the hallway to the other, convicts hung on hooks in the walls and waited to be prestidigitated by the Law. Most of them hung there without incident, docile, eyes glazed over, limbs flaccid. Whenever a convict made trouble or got wise, he was dealt with posthaste, sometimes by an officer with a fusion baton, sometimes by the surveillance system, which had an itchy

29

trigger finger and always looked for an excuse to violate some asshole's civil liberties and right to due process.

Among the plainclothes and copper-plated officers that rushed up and down the hallway lingered the occasional piece of livestock. Cows, mainly. But also swine, fowl, goats, sheep. The animals had been genetically enhanced and treated with growth hormones. Some chickens stood over five feet tall. On their hind legs, some pigs approached eight feet. Unfamiliars often feared for their lives. The livestock's emotional and somatic sensoria had been plucked, though, ensuring that none of them got in bad moods and commenced people-eating rampages.

In one room, a deep, horrified oink...

In the next room, an interrogation turned grisly. Fruity Pebbles poured out of the victim's wounds...

In the next room, a Jim Carrey robot with red Riddler hair impersonating a CSI David Caruso clone took off its sunglasses and squinted at a docket, said, "Mark my words, ladies and gentlemen," put on its sunglasses and looked at the ceiling light, took off its sunglasses and squinted at the docket, said, "That's all she wrote, boys and girls," put on its sunglasses and looked at the ceiling light, took off its sunglasses and squinted at the docket, said, "Here comes the Big Hurt, folks," put on its sunglasses and...

In the next room, an assistant to the deputy chief's second lieutenant's sixth vice principal of Purloined Letter memorabilia sang a Barry Manilow ballad to an audience of blank-faced colleagues who slurped coffee and fingered donuts...

In the next room...

Codename Vincent Prague burst in as if shot from a cannon. He flew headfirst across a table, smashed into a wall, bounced off it, somersaulted backwards across the table, and disappeared out the door. The door slammed behind him. A suspect crouched before the table. Two detectives stood on either side of him. A giant sheep stood in the corner.

All of the interrogation room's occupants idly watched Prague enter and exit...

Prague came back in, shut the door and locked it. "What's the charge," he droned. He wore a scramble suit that projected over 100,000 physiognomic fraction-representations of photographs, sketches, illustrations and caricatures of pulp science fiction author Philip K. Dick onto its superthin, shroudlike membrane. The effekt was simple enough: you never knew which Dick you were dealing with.

"What the hell is that?" said one of the detectives.

"An allusion," replied Prague. "Or plagiarism. Same thing in this case, perhaps." He grinned. "Pardon me. I haven't had any coffee today. Don't even talk to me if I haven't had any coffee."

"Who the hell are you?" said the other detective. The sheep baaed.

Shaking his head, Prague unzipped the scramble suit and shrugged and stepped out of it. Beneath he wore a Philip K Dick flab suit. The suit was extremely lifelike and adequately represented the author at the height of his chubbiest, drugged out years: high forehead, giant face, piercing blue eyes, vulture's nest beard, barrel chest, disproportionate spare tire around the waist, cheap shirt, cheap pants, flip-flops, and a self-refillable snuff box collar that constantly stuffed tobacco into his nostrils with thin mechanical arms.

The detectives looked at each other. The suspect said, "Is he going to kill me?"

"That's enough outta you, goodfella." Prague slammed his fist into a wall. He grabbed the table and hurled it aside. He picked the suspect up by the scruff and shoved his nose in his face. "Answer me! Answer me you stinking douche bag!"

"You d-didn't ask me a question!" The snuff collar misread noses and shoved a pinch of tobacco into the suspect's nostrils. He cried out. He sneezed. Prague threw him back into the chair. The detectives told Prague he was out of line. Not only that, he didn't even know the charge—by his own admittance. Prague said he knew enough. He proceeded to play badcop/goodcop by himself, screaming at and punching the suspect one moment, then smiling, speaking softly, and massaging him. He oscillated back and forth between cops four times before the detectives restrained him. He let them.

He removed the PKD flab suit.

"Mr Prague!" exclaimed a detective. "We're so sorry. We didn't know it was you." His partner handed him a pen and paper and asked for an autograph. Prague obligingly scribbled it down:

# Beep Beep!

The detective frowned at the autograph. His partner invited Prague to stay for lunch. "We were just about to eat," he said. "Please do join us. It would be our honor." The other detective agreed. Prague replied evenly: "I eat alone." But they wouldn't hear of it. Rolling up their sleeves, they pistolwhipped and cuffed the suspect to a radiator, brandished gigantic butcher knives, and fell on the sheep...

It took a while for the animal to die. Longer than Prague expected. The detectives kept missing their mark. It came as no surprise considering the ridiculously unbridled abandon with which they executed their task. They chopped off its tail, its hind legs, its snout. Once or twice they nearly chopped off each other's appendages.

The sheep's incisive, high-pitched scream shattered the interrogation room's two-way mirror, exposing a guilty-looking janitor on the other side. The janitor ducked out of view...

The sheep flailed and convulsed and tried to crawl away, pulling itself onward with its forelegs, bleeding real blood. The detectives studied the blood. Prague studied the detectives.

The sheep went faster. Soon it pulled itself in circles around the room at an impressive speed.

Panicking, the detectives hacked at it indiscriminately. They missed every time, the wide blades of their knives clattering against the concrete floor. Prague marveled at their inability to make contact. He knew toddlers that had better aim.

Finally Prague put the sheep out of its misery. He pulled out a supersized F/X pistol, leveled it at the sheep, and fired...The sheep's head exploded in Technicolor. Vivid pastels and gaudy chromatics marked the fountain of brain and skull and veins that blossomed upwards, reaching for the ceiling at an increasingly slower pace...The gruesome pyrotechnics freeze-framed for one... two...three beats...then imploded in fasttime.

The headless sheep continued to move forward for a few seconds before lying still.

Prague holstered his firearm. "Poor sonofabitch," he said.

"Sheep brains are a delicacy," said the detectives in tandem. "What's the matter with you?" They wiped the blood on their hands onto stiff white shirts.

Prague puffed out his cheeks. "Same thing's the matter with everybody, I guess. Not enough green tea in my diet." He never understood the concept of privatized carnivorism, especially in that it only applied to civil servants. Was requiring civil servants by Law to kill and prepare their own meat an attempt on the government's part to discourage citizens from the profession? Or was it meant to encourage them? Either way made as much sense as nonsense. At any rate, Prague elected to be a vegetarian from the very beginning of his employment. Not because he didn't like meat. He was simply too lazy, hygienic and smug to prepare meat.

The detectives didn't forgive Prague for his hastiness easily and presented him with a Two Minute Hate that included everything from offended glares to loud, inventive trills of cursing and gesticulating. Prague took what they dished out, hoping they would lay a hand on him. No luck. After the Hate concluded, all was well. They apologized and shook Prague's hand and slapped him on the back and took turns pistolwhipping the suspect to make sure he was still unconscious and dewooled the sheep's torso with stylish rust-textured retrofutique vibronic shears and skinned the sheep with vintage Rambo knives and stripped off its flesh with their bare hands. A third detective entered the interrogation room wheeling in a long barrel grill and complaining about a propane monger who had sabotaged the reserve of hydrogen-cell grills. He poured in a sack of charcoal. He doused the charcoal with lighter fluid. He tried to light the charcoal with a match. It wouldn't light. He tried again. It wouldn't light. He lit the entire matchbook on fire and threw it in the grill. It went out.

"Goddamn it!"

"What's the problem?" The other detectives joined him at the grill and fiddled with its many useless knobs.

Curiosity dwindled sharply into boredom. "Can you rozzes tell me where Commodore Rabelais's office is?" Prague said. "It used to be in here. Where's the fucker at?"

The detectives looked over their shoulders at him as if he were a stranger. "Rabelais?" said one of them. "The General Assistant Managerial Choreographer of Mortal Affairs for the Ministry of Applied Pressure's Department of Anthropologism? He's a Klamm. He doesn't work in this slaughterhouse. This slaughterhouse's nothing but Lowrys. Always has been, far as I know. Isn't that right?" He looked at his colleagues. Oblivious, they returned to the grill.

Thanking the detectives, Prague adjusted the F/X pistol to the seventh, highest setting (a.k.a. the ROSHWALD notch) and fired it at the sheep's mangled body. A surge of radioactive green flames consumed the body and its flesh decayed in a vivid, putrid timelapse that featured prehistoric grub worms, eighteen gallons of spurting auxiliary blood, and a bevy of internal organs that screamed from random improvised orifices. The residual skeleton looked spit-shined; it glowed in the muted light of the interrogation room. The detectives, on the other hand, were barely perceptible beneath the thick swathes of gore that caked them from fedora to flatfeet...

# 02
## The Case of the Errant Bottle of Carbonated Olive Oil

All stories begin with a first sentence. This story is just like all the others...

Doktor Hermann Teufelsdröckh opened a bottle of olive oil. It fizzed and exploded like a shook up beer.

He read the label...*Carbonated* olive oil?

He growled for the assistants.

Hadn't he told them to buy non-carbonated olive oil? Yes. Of course he had. Why would he ask them to buy carbonated olive oil? Under no conceivable circumstance would he employ it. The fact that carbonated olive oil even existed was stupid. Other than a novelty item, it had no rationale. And what was really so novel about it? People had been carbonating things for ages. Just because somebody carbonated something that didn't deserve to be carbonated made it unique? *Stierscheiße*. They might as well have carbonated chicken noodle soup. Or chicken, for that matter. Or a shoe. The modern world was a practical joke. Dr Teufelsdröckh realized this sad fact of life more and more every day. Yet all he could do was play along. That's all anybody could do.

The assistants didn't respond to him. He looked around the kitchen. He was sure he had just seen them two minutes ago. What had they been doing? Dicing vegetables. No, emptying the dishwasher. No, stomping on light bulbs. No, playing Monopoly...Did he send them back to the grocery store already? For what? He sent them to the grocery store on several occasions every day. Sometimes it was difficult to keep track why. What had he sent them out for earlier? Sun-dried tomatoes. Then, a few minutes later, leeks. Then, minutes later, tofu. Then dill weed. Then bulghur pilaf. Then a turnip. Then farfalline pasta. Then taglliatelle pasta. Then gnocchetti sardi pasta. Then wasabe. Then sage. Then poi. Then artichoke relish. Then ostrich egg yolks. Then sauvignon blanc. Then Gerolsteiner. Then jicama. Then portabella mushrooms. Then chili peppers. Then scallions. Then tea leaves...Was that all?

"Truth! Beauty!"

They blustered into the kitchen, fighting over a bag of parsnips.

The assistants were pathological effekts of a failed allegory. Dr Teufelsdröckh hired them two years ago when his old assistants realized they could make more than minimum wage in healthier professions. To avoid another episode of identity-assertion, he included stipulations in the new assistants' contracts mandating that they change their names to Truth and Beauty and consequently emulate these notions in terms of image, fashion, conduct, and ideally psyche (although determining if the assistants consistently represented their names in their respective mental diegeses was a nearly impossible task in the absence of quality psychoforensics equipment). Essentially they were an experiment in Keatsian sociopoetics to see if the assistants would function as identical organisms on multiple plateaus of existence and prove that, as Keats claimed in his poem "Ode on a Grecian Urn," "Beauty is truth, truth is beauty—that is all ye know on earth, and all ye need to know." Needless to say, the experiment failed, and their contracts had to be rewritten. The assistants were as different as two different people strapped into a difference engine. They had no manners either, regardless of being forced to view and review *My Fair Lady* (for examples of proper conduct) and the Sergio Leone canon (for examples of improper conduct). In addition, Truth was not truthful. He was a goddamn liar. And Beauty was ugly. Still, they remained in Dr Teufelsdröckh's service under the auspices of despicable wages as well as absurdist demands and expectations. Despite himself, he couldn't complain.

Truth kicked Beauty between the legs. Beauty keeled over. Truth caught the parsnips before they hit the floor and ran them over to Dr Teufelsdröckh.

"Thank you, Truth." He took the parsnips. "But that wasn't very friendly. Your partner is your comrade. Your comrade is your cohort. Your cohort is your right hand man. Your right hand man is your co-worker. Your co-worker is your colleague. You can arrange those terms any way you like. They all mean the same thing."

Truth nodded. "I understand," he lied.

Dr Teufelsdröckh knew he was lying. He let it pass. "Fine. Now give Beauty a hand, please. It's one thing to crack a man in the nuts. It's quite another thing to leave him in your dust."

Confused, Truth placed a finger on his chin in an attempt to look contemplative. He maintained this stance as Beauty got up, staggered across the kitchen, and sidled next to him, massaging his groin.

"Well done, Beauty." Dr Teufelsdröckh sighed and shook his head. A general air of unsightliness marked Beauty's character in the form of outsized facial features (big nose, big ears, big cheeks, big Adam's apple) and a round-shouldered, undernourished physique. Two features, however, stood out and undermined his would-be vocational name. First, a set of chapped lips. They were hard and cracked and seemed to have been overcooked by a desert sun, and when he spoke, the lips rubbed together like little chunks of asphalt. The second feature, his eyebrows—they were even more irksome. Complete opposites, one eyebrow, which resembled an obese caterpillar, appeared to be the doppelgänger of the other, which was pencil-thin. Dr Teufelsdröckh often accused Beauty of manicuring the pencil-thin eyebrow, secretively whittling it down from its originary bulk. But Beauty claimed the eyebrow was a natural formation. Whatever the case, the doktor sent the assistant to physiognomic detox his first day on the job. His entire face was reconstructed in the pristine, well-groomed, utopian image of John Keats himself. The surgery didn't take, however, and Beauty's face devolved back to its primal form in a matter of weeks, as if laughing at Dr Teufelsdröckh for trying to do away with it. Beauty himself never smiled, let alone laughed. But his face told another story.

Dr Teufelsdröckh opened the bag and sniffed the parsnips. They smelled vaguely unripe. Not to their detriment, though. They would do.

He set the parsnips aside. "Right. Now to the matter at hand. Now, I say, to the matter of carbonated olive oil..."

Beauty remained silent during the subsequent invective, partly because he focused on nursing his genitals back to health, mostly because he thought he deserved the invective. Truth, on the other hand, butted in. "The thing is," he kept saying. Every time he said it, Dr Teufelsdröckh waited for him to go on, but he never did. Dr Teufelsdröckh could have brought the issue to light, but that's precisely what Truth wanted, he suspected, so he permitted the interruptions, clearing his throat and wetting his lips with his tongue whenever they occurred. He would not give in to Truth. Unlike his fellow assistant, looking at him was not a distasteful experience, even though he was equally diminutive, but diminution, as the doktor saw it, whether physical or psychological (usually both), was the *cri du coeur* of any assistant's *Dasein*. Not to say that Truth wasn't distasteful. Virtually everything he did made his employer want to flog him with an incineration rod. He couldn't even tolerate being in the same room with Truth. Yet he tolerated Truth. All the time. And that's another reason why he didn't fire him. Truth reliably put Dr Teufelsdröckh's patience to the test, challenging the strength of his social character. It was a challenge he both valued and needed inasmuch as he believed the insignia of a fully developed gentleman, above all else, consisted of an unfaltering ability to negotiate horseshit and assholery at every turn.

Dr Teufelsdröckh's voice began to crackle and skip as he continued to reprimand the assistants and cope with Truth's stoppages. He poured himself a tall glass of table wine and paused to take sips and grease his larynx. It wasn't long before the sips overtook his dialogue. Soon he had washed down two glasses and was halfway through a third, swishing the wine around his mouth, checking the legs on the bulb of the glass, rubbing his tongue across his hard palate, meditating on the different flavors he detected in the wine...

Silence.

Truth said, "You told us to buy carbonated olive oil."

No visible response at first. Then Dr Teufelsdröckh convulsed. "What's that you say?" he blubbered.

"He said you told us to buy carbonated olive oil," said Beauty.

Dr Teufelsdröckh spit a mouthful of wine into the sink. "I'm going to pretend I didn't hear that." He swallowed the remainder of wine in the glass and, pouring himself another glass, said, "But let's assume that what you say is true. Let's assume it. For the sake of argument. You say—*both* of you say—that I told you to buy carbonated olive oil. Fine. That's what you say. That's what you're telling me that I told you to do, and you do what I tell you to do, because I tell you to do it, and because I pay you to do it. In short, that is the nature of your occupation, or, as it were, your *job*. Now then. Here is the question I want to pose and, if you will, problematize. Why would I ask you to purchase carbonated olive oil? That's the question. That's the question I'm talking about. Here's another one: What can a man do with carbonated olive oil? What can anyone do with it? Why does it even exist, is the thing I really want to know. Have you ever heard of a meal of any genre, class or ethnicity that features carbonated olive oil as a requisite ingredient? Have you ever even heard of anybody dipping a piece of bread into carbonated olive oil for the sake of a pleasurable tasting experience? Don't say you have, because you haven't—because nobody has."

"The thing is," said Truth.

The doktor took a sharp sip of wine. "As far as I know, the only thing you can do with carbonated olive oil is drink it straight from the bottle. Do you know what else you can drink straight from a bottle? Milk. Piss. Hemlock. Whatever you damn well want. But you don't use it to cook a meal! Hence my point. Thus and so. You understand, yes? But let's pretend you don't understand. Which you clearly don't. In which case we won't be pretending anything. On the contrary, we will be operating within the confines of *reality*, per se. Which is to say, reality is performative by *nature*. Which is to say, whatever we accomplish here, whatever we *do*, be it known that our actions are not natural or free-spirited, as some Nerf mongers would have it. An action is an *act*, after all, as in *to act*, as in *to play a role*. Man is a histrionic, technological animal. And nature is the theater of technology." Sip of wine. "At this point I'd like to revert back to my thesis. What was I talking about, for Christ's sake?" Sip of wine. Sip of wine...

Beauty started to nod off. Truth killed a ladybug that landed on his arm.

Dr Teufelsdröckh chewed a fingernail. "Yes, olive oil. Meals. I'm making a meal, you see. This is the point. I'm making a meal, and it calls for olive oil, *not* carbonated olive oil, which is an atrocity, which is something that could only exist in a shitty pulp novel or B-movie, and yet here I sit in my kitchen, and over there, sitting on the countertop, is a gigantic bottle of carbonated olive oil. I realize that olive oil, carbonated or not, is still olive oil. But when one says olive oil, when one *thinks* olive oil, the last thing that comes to mind is carbonation. So here's the score. Either we are all characters in a shitty pulp novel or B-movie, or else you, my assistants, have committed an act of idiocy. I hope you can hear me. Am I making myself clear?"

Truth handed Dr Teufelsdröckh a slip of paper.

"What's this?" He snatched the paper. Scribbled on it were the items he had asked his assistants to purchase for him that day...Sun-dried tomatoes. Leeks. Tofu. Dill weed. Bulgur pilaf. A turnip. One pasta after another...The last item on the list was, apropos, a bottle of **CARBONATED** olive oil, beneath which hung a subcategory listing acceptable brands.

Truth said, "I thought it was an odd request."

Beauty said, "An odd request."

Truth said, "That's what I say. So I made sure to underline the word *carbonated* and put it in bold print and capital letters on my grocery list. That way, when we got to the grocery store, I wouldn't rethink what you may or may not have told us to buy. What I mean is, I wouldn't think that what I wrote down might have been a mistake, even though I only write down what you tell me and I've never made a mistake before. But you never know."

Beauty said, "It's difficult to know things, sometimes."

Truth said, "That's what I say. The only way to really be sure about things is to write them down. And the more detailed you are when you write things down, the better. The word **CARBONATED** on my grocery list is an example of extreme detail. There's no questioning it. There's no denying it. It's big and black and underlined."

Beauty said, "Like an ocean at midnight if you look at the ocean upside-down."

Truth looked askance at Beauty. "I'm not sure about that simile. I'm not sure if it works. I don't even think it makes sense."

Beauty said, "It makes sense to me."

Truth said, "Everything makes sense to you. You're like a—"

"Enough!" The doktor finished his glass of wine, stared at the glass for a moment, and then hurled it across the kitchen. It shattered against the pantry door. A Mr Clean robot in white T-shirt and jeans exited a closet and cleaned and sterilized the mess with multipurpose mechanical arms. The robot bowed and returned to the closet, its white eyes burning brightly around two almost imperceptible black pupils.

The assistants looked willfully at Dr Teufelsdröckh. "I'm not quite sure where to begin," he said, feeling unable to holster the temper tantrum that welled up in him. "I suppose I should point out that merely writing something down does not ensure its truthfulness, and it certainly doesn't mean I said it. Do I even have to say this aloud?" He paused. He clicked his jaw. "Let me just say... Good afternoon. I'm uncertain why you have elected to victimize and sabotage me. I'm not the best employer. I'm aware of that. I'm aware. But I'm not the worst employer either—far from it. Etcetera. Viz., and so forth." Retrieving another bottle of wine from a cupboard, Dr Teufelsdröckh exited the kitchen, abandoning the soufflé he had intended to make himself for dinner.

Beauty peered at Truth. "You're scheming on a thing," he droned. "That's sabotage."

Truth rearranged his lips...

Dr Teufelsdröckh strode down a hallway, slid open an oily chain-link fence and stepped into an elevator. He threw a switch. The elevator clanked and grumbled to life.

"Lah-bor-ah-tory."

The slow descent took five minutes. On the way, he considered the prospect that Truth had actually been telling the truth. Truth almost always lied, but for the sake of speculation, he pretended that he didn't almost always lie, or rather, he put faith in the small percentage of Truth's character that wasn't a dissembler. He didn't like the prospect. It meant that he had deliberately requested carbonated olive oil, a request that had no *raison d'être*. Perhaps he had been thinking about carbonation. Had he dreamt of carbonation the night before? Had the idea of carbonation leaked from his unconscious into his preconscious mind, then sidestepped his conscious mind and surfaced in his discourse? If so, what were the chances that carbonation would emerge in his discourse precisely when he conceived to utter (and then uttered) the words "olive oil." Preposterous. Absurd. And yet not impossible. He recalled drinking a certain variety of club soda that resonated with his palate. When had he sipped that club soda? Only last week. Clearly he had been preoccupied with the club soda. Clearly he had not forgotten what it had done to him.

Sometimes he wished there was a hole. A hole without principle, merit, significance or dynamism that formed where something else used to be. It came from nowhere. It led nowhere. It did nothing.

He might climb into that hole and disappear forever...

By the time the elevator clattered to a halt, Dr Teufelsdröckh had convinced himself that Truth was telling the truth, at least in the case regarding the errant bottle of carbonated olive oil, while in the kitchen, Truth explained to Beauty just how one commits a true act of idiocy.

"Lights."

The laboratory came alive with a hydraulic grandeur, with ticking clocks, vibrating wires, glass tubes of canned voltage running from floor to ceiling, whistling pipes and pan-flutes, swinging levers and light bulbs, streamlined aquariums teeming with sturgeon and suckfish, Bunsen burners the size of torch lamps, purple and red and blue and yellow spotlights, test tubes and beakers and percolators and vials that frothed and bubbled, ergometers, enameled pedals, discs and balls, homunculi that crossed and recrossed their eyes pickled in great jars...The technologized rattle and hum clashed with the sound of a sentient theater organ that played and replayed the overture from Andrew Lloyd Weber's *Phantom of the Opera*. A long wallscreen ran fasttime footage of *Frankenstein* adaptations and offshoots, skidding into slowtime only when a mad scientist exclaimed, "It's aaaalliiiiiiiiiiiiiiiiiiiiiiiiiiivve!" The footage oscillated between monochrome and Technicolor...

Grinning, Dr Teufelsdröckh stepped into a pair of crab slippers that delivered him to the opposite end of the room where a red velvet curtain had been draped over what might have been a hat rack, or a floor lamp, or a mailbox. He ran his fingers over the delicate fabric of the curtain. Then he clenched the curtain and yanked it aside.

...The skin of the stick figure was black—so black it seemed two-dimensional. And yet its body clearly possessed depth. There were no features. There were no fingers or toes. Its gender was difficult to place; the figure lacked genitals and looked androgynous. Something about it, though, was altogether human. Or rather, more human than human. Or, as the doktor liked to think, more human than more human than human (and, in some senses, even more human than that).

He placed a hand on the stick figure's chest as if to feel its heartbeat, then leaned over and whispered something into its tympanic membrane. Static electricity played on his lips.

# 03
## Interview with a MAP Man

SAMSA. Syncretic Amerikan Metaformulaic Stock Agent.

There were SAMSAs everywhere.

Vincent Prague dodged a charging bull as he strode down the hallway. He was taller than the SAMSAs and saw the animal coming, so he had plenty of time to duck out of the way. Shoulder-to-shoulder traffic in the hallway, though, and he tripped and fell...Somebody caught him. SAMSA...067. That's what his hat claimed, anyway.

Prague said, "They got you up and running again already? I kicked your ass two seconds ago. These weird bastards are quick."

"Quick is a frame of mind, Mr Prague," said the SAMSA icily. "I see you've managed to—"

The SAMSA was ripped from Prague's line of vision as a horn pierced his chest and another bull carried him away...

...Prague kicked open the door. Its hinges came off and the door sailed across the office and slammed into a glass trophy cabinet, shattering it.

Commodore Rabelais sprung to his feet. His knees knocked against the edge of his desk. He fell back into his chair. He doubled-over and vanished beneath the desk.

Prague scratched an Achilles tendon with the toe of his opposing shoe.

Moaning, Cdre Rabelais crawled back into the chair and stared at Prague as if he had murdered his children. "*Scheiße!* Do you how much a nice door costs? What's the matter with you? *Scheiße!*" He pushed a button and reported the damage. A swarm of nanomites flowed into the office through a ceiling vent and ate the door on the floor. Two SAMSAs in orange jumpsuits appeared and installed a fresh door while a mouth in the wall opened and sucked in the smashed trophy case—sound of imploding wood and metal—and then spit out a new trophy case. A SAMSA speedswept the floor, placed a receipt on Rabelais's desk, and left. Everything was back to normal in under a minute.

Massaging his knees, Rabelais said, "That expense is coming out of your ass. I don't joke about doors. Here." He held out the receipt. Prague took it and stuffed it in his pocket. "Trophy cases are another matter," continued the Commodore. "Particularly when they're decorative. Particularly when they're for show. Doors have use-value. Doors open and close and so forth."

"I see," said Prague.

Rabelais huffed. "Do you? I wonder sometimes. I wonder if you see anything."

"Well, you know what they say about perception. Perception is a daunting mosaic of catacombs down which the hairy members of anonymity flow like a—"

"Can the birdshit, Vinnie. No time. All told, I'm glad you're here, even if you're late." He stood again and walked out from behind the desk. Rabelais's attire surprised Prague. Instead of a standard-issue UMU (Upper Management Uniform), he wore a forgettable business suit. He almost looked like a SAMSA. But he looked more like a scarecrow with his big head in the shape of an overinflated paper bag. And Prague could still fit the little creep in his britches.

"Somebody die?" Prague chirped. "What's with the shiteating threads?"

Rabelais smiled. "It's Friday," he said. He didn't say anything else.

Prague shrugged. "I was gonna dress up for you. But I got sidetracked. I don't feel like dressing up anymore. Costumes dictate performativity, if only in spirit, and I'm just not in a performative mood."

"That's magnificent," he replied through a slit of mouth. "Are you finished? Have a seat. Talking to you is exhausting. A little bit of smartass goes a long way. Too much ends up nowhere." A sentient chair crawled across the office floor and tapped Prague on the thigh. Prague rolled his eyes as the chair struck him in the back of the knees, breaking his stance, and cradled him into a sitting position.

"There we are." Rabelais returned to his chair and lit a cigar the size of a baby's arm. Taking an egregious puff, he tapped a sheet of paper on the desk. "Congratulations Mr Anvil-in-Chief. This is your assignment. First, however, you'll have to excuse me. It's been over fifteen minutes. At least."

The Commodore uttered something into an intercom in a derivation of Noirspeak that Prague didn't recognize. He spoke five derivations himself, but there were over sixty in City City alone, each as different from the next as apples and Agent Orange.

Another mouth opened in a wall and coughed two zombies into the corner of the office. They were stock Romero zombies that smarted of wax figures more than the real McCoy: flashy glamrock makeup, jointless limbs, foam latex bite wounds and slash marks and rotting flesh...At first they petted, fondled and tapped each other, like wrestlers getting a sense of the opposition. Before long they graduated to cannibalism and ripping off limbs. Green slime sprayed out of one zombie, white mucous out of the other. The battle culminated with an exhibition of furious brain eating after which the victorious zombie tore off its own growling head and cracked it open on its knee. Stinking maggots, roaches and eels exploded from the rupture and the zombie's body melted into a pool of hot sludge. Rabelais squeaked in ecstasy...

As always, the slaughterhouse's ardent janitorial lackeys cleaned up the bloodbath at record-breaking speed. They also provided Rabelais with a fresh pair of undergarments and suit pants.

Prague looked on blankly, sighing and shifting in his chair as it all came back to him. Interviews with Rabelais were prolonged and tedious. What should have taken five minutes took fifty, especially given the Commodore's voyeuristic addiction to ultraviolence. Day and night, he needed to witness some form of over-the-top butchery at regular intervals. Failure to do this educed disorders ranging from apoplectic fits to unruly psychotic interludes. TV was insufficient. Lucid dreams were insufficient. Pharmaceuticals didn't work. Ultraviolence needed to be enacted in real life (and at close range) for Rabelais to temporarily suppress the strange flows of his desires. In general, the disorder manifested in Tier One citizens who could afford enough androids on an hourly basis to keep themselves in balance. It was almost unheard of in government employees. But Rabelais's connections were deep and wide.

"One leg at a time," remarked the Commodore as he put on the new pants. They zipped and buckled themselves. He sat back down and retrieved his cigar. He admired the ember. "This is a fine cigar. I insist on smoking fine cigars."

Prague studied his lap.

"Wake up!"

Prague flinched. "Who's there?"

"Your boss, Hamlet." He leaned back in his chair. "Did you know 'Who's there?' is the opening line of *Hamlet*? Did you know that I know every opening line of every Shakespearean play by rote? R-O-T-E. Every play can be analyzed *in extremis* through the filter of its opening line. In *Hamlet*, for instance, 'Who's there?' introduces, first of all, an element of mystery, of something unseen, perhaps nonexistent, yet *present*, if only in the mind of the player who speaks the words, who is *on guard*, if you will, literally, as he is a guard by vocation. This initial reading is deepened when we recognize that it is night and the guard speaks into the darkness, a foreboding setting for obvious reasons, viz., night and darkness symbolize death, misery, horror, dread, and so forth. Ultimately the guard's query signifies a rift between what may appear to be real and what is actually real—in other words, between reality and fantasy, between the world of consciousness and dreams. In that moment, the guard can't discriminate between one and the other, not until his partner answers him and moves into the light of his torch. It is this very moment that holds the diagnostic key to the rest of the play. To varying degrees, the same can be said for all of Shakespeare's plays. Which means that there's no reason to read the plays. It would be a waste of time. All one needs to read are the opening lines. In fact, anybody who reads more than the first line of a Shakespearean play is a fool, in fact."

"You said 'in fact' twice."

There was a long silence.

Rabelais leaned forward and tapped the paper on his desk again. "As I was saying, your assignment." He clenched the cigar with his teeth. "You are to leave City City this instant and fly to the city of Prague in the Former Czech

Republik. FYI I'm aware of the irony that your questionable self-designated codename happens to coincide with the name of your destination. I assure you, it's purely coincidental, although you'll discover that this irony will be exacerbated by the fact that you are to go to the Hotel Prague on Prague Street and contact a bellhop named Henrí Prague who will usher you up to your room, the Galactic Pot-Healer Suite, and introduce you to his sister, Mädchen "The Prague" Prague. She will serve you breakfast and run you a hot bath. Then she will escort you to a discotheque called The Delova Prague beneath which is a casino called Pragensia St Cagney. At this point you are to play Yahtzee and wait for further instructions." A mechanical arm reached out of the desktop, took the Commodore's cigar, tapped it over an ash tray, and returned it to his mouth. "Oh yes," he added. "One last thing. Here." He removed something from a drawer and threw it at Prague...a T-shirt. Prague took it by the shoulders and let it fall open. Inscribed onto the front was a CGI version of Vincent Prague in a Boy Scout uniform—yellow scarf, sash with merit badges, short shorts, knee-high socks—administering the three-finger salute. Beneath the image were four words: **My Name Is Prague**. Prague regarded Rabelais acidly. Rabelais laughed. "Just kidding. Let's have it back, then. We need it for a belated Halloween party they're throwing this evening in Slaughterhouse-Nine." The mechanical arm reached across the desk and snatched away the T-shirt. Prague made a face. Rabelais said, "When you introduced me to your codename, I was less than pleased, admittedly. Less than pleased, mind you. But the codename has grown on me in the last few hours, so much that presently I don't think a more awe-inspiring codename has ever bore its shining meathead in the history of MAP affairs. I'm not sure if you were joking or being serious when you conceived of it. Whatever the case, you know the rules—spies can pick their own codenames. Doesn't make much sense to me. Then again, neither does my wife's cooking. Neither does day and night, for that matter. Any questions? Concerns? You're the Anvil-in-Chief now. Don't let us down."

Prague did his best to keep his cool and breathe evenly. A difficult task. The MAP had fucked him over more than once. They'd fuck him over again.

Not to mention his boss's eccentricities and terrific longwindedness. But being in the cut was all he knew. And it was all he ever wanted to do.

He had been to Prague before, once, as a child. His parents were Kafka fetishists and took him there to visit the author's house-cum-museum/bookstore/café. He remembered the address: No. 22 Golden Lane. He remembered what color the house had been painted on the outside: tropical sky blue. He remembered the smell on the inside of the house: a rank crossbreed of overcooked sauerkraut and dusty, weathered hardbacks. He remembered the figure in the corner of the main room: a genetic reincarnation of a moribund 44-year-old Kafka, petrified, naked but for a bowler hat, his skin injected with a clearcoat plasma that allowed tourists to view the horror of his tubercular innards. And he remembered flying into the city itself, a heaving and dynamic clot of towers and cathedrals and basilicas, their pointed rooftops defined by great swords that pierced an emphatic, hissing blanket of overlying fog and mist...

As for being Anvil-in-Chief, Prague could care less. Like all titles, this one was as empty as an overturned fedora. He said, "What sort of funding can I expect for this gig?" He knew the answer to the question before he asked it. But he asked it.

"Funding?" Rabelais cackled. He stopped cackling, then resumed with greater intensity. "That's funny, Vinnie!" He choked on his tongue. In a deadpan voice, he said, "But of course funding is your concern. As always, you may or may not be reimbursed, compensated and promoted depending on the degree of the mission's success or failure."

"Blah fucking blah."

"Indeed. Excuse me."

This time a nine foot sasquatch and a Dolph Lundgren clone squared off. The Lundgren had on Masters of the Universe regalia and boasted an anabolic physique and Sword of Power. The sasquatch immediately slapped the sword from its grip, however, and they engaged full-throttle in hand-to-hand combat. The Lundgren went straight for the balls. The sasquatch balked but the blow didn't faze it and it retaliated with a clumsy judo throw—*hiza garuma*, Prague calculated—that swept its opponent off its feet and flipped it a full 360 degrees.

The Lundgren landed on its feet. Both fighters cocked their heads in disbelief. The Lundgren kicked the sasquatch in the knee. Cdre Rabelais narrowed his eyes and groaned at the sound of the knee shattering like a light bulb. As the sasquatch doubled over, it caught the Lundgren's head and twisted it, cracking the neck and hacking off its aquiline nose with a claw. The Lundgren continued to fight with its head facing the opposite direction. They punched each other for two minutes. Then the sasquatch disemboweled the Lundgren, tearing open the android's six pack and yanking out intestines hand over fist. There was no blood. Only viscera. And the viscera scarcely glistened in the dull orange light of the office.

Rabelais clutched his chest. "Cunt on a stick! These models are supposed to be fully loaded. The government isn't paying for me to get off on empty shells." The sasquatch looked at him with wet, apologetic eyes. Rabelais retrieved an instruction manual from a drawer and began to rifle through it.

A SAMSA entered the office through a trap door and brained the sasquatch with a two-by-four. As the cleaning crew busied themselves, Prague rose from his chair. The chair tried to keep him seated, but he eluded it.

"This has been fun, CR. Go fuck yourself."

"Relax, Vinnie," he said, setting the manual aside. "No need to get pissy now."

"I'm not pissy. I'm cool. I'm calm. I'm Jack and the beanstalk."

Rabelais nodded. "OK. Not sure what beanstalks have to do with the price of beans. Solid fairy tale, though. Same thing goes for fairy tales as for Shakespeare, by the way. All literature, really."

"Thanks for the tip. Ibid, fuck you."

"More pissiness. Where does it end?"

The chair's arm reached up and gripped Prague by the elbow. He ripped off the arm, then turned and destroyed the chair with a fusillade of stomps.

"You're paying for that," said Rabelais.

Prague replied, "If you say so. I'll be in touch. Maybe I'll oblige the MAP after all—killing that chair brings back memories."

As he left, the wall birthed a mob of xenophobic, sadistic Karen Carpenters and one occupant of interplanetary flesh...

# 04
## The Scorsese Boys

After receiving his assignment, Anvil-in-Chief Vincent Prague went straight to the zoo and stole a crocodile. "People usually try to stay clear of crocs," said the zookeeper when he watched the tape of the theft. "They don't befriend them."

Prague put a leash on the crocodile and took it on a walk through the park. It devoured two dogs. It attacked a toddler in a stroller.

Prague apologized to the toddler's mother. He apologized to the crocodile before putting it down with a gyrostabilized submachine gun. "You're riding high in April," he told a reporter, "shot down in May." He signed a few autographs, then went home to pack. He wouldn't tell Rabelais that he planned on taking the job until later. Maybe he wouldn't tell him at all.

On the gondola ride, he put on a halo and skimmed the editorials that spiraled around his head. The other passengers did likewise, sitting at attention in hoverchairs, backs straight, hands on knees, with lips granulated like scar tissue...Beyond the gondola, the lights of City City slashed the night into long strips of chemical darkness...

Prague ran into trouble outside the entranceway to his building. It set in motion a sequence of troubling events that encompassed nearly two decades of his life.

The Scorsese Boys.

They included the meanest, craziest and most vicious of director Martin Scorsese's anti-heros: *Casino*'s Nicky Santoro, *Gangs of New York*'s Bill the Butcher, *Cape Fear*'s Max Cady, *GoodFellas* Tommy DeVito, *The Departed*'s

Francis Costello, and *Taxi Driver*'s Travis Bickle. All of the androids were easily recognizable by their roles and the actors who played them. Prague was well-versed in Scorsese cinema and had scrapped with the gangsters before. The MAP unleashed them whenever they suspected an agent of insubordination, even if the act of insubordination had not yet occurred, and even if the probability of it occurring was a shot in the dark.

The Scorsese Boys annoyed Prague on multiple levels. The shithawking terrorism they wreaked annoyed him, of course, but so did the fact that DeVito and Santoro, both of which had originally been portrayed by Joe Pesci, looked almost exactly alike except for discrepancies in fashion. Prague liked to be able to tell the difference between things. Additionally, the Scorsese Boys all wanted to be Travis Bickle and resented the fact that they weren't. Every non-Bickle android tried to talk and act like the taxi driver, despite being inhibited by its own pre-programmed accent and mannerisms. Prague had a low tolerance for that sort of flâneury. Even from a robot.

"Who let this rat motherfucker in my town?" said the Costello. "Somebody says you gotta Jones wit da Man."

"Jones?" said Prague. "You mean I wanna smoke the Man?"

"You talkin' to me?" the Bickle responded, glancing over its shoulders. The rest of the Scorsese Boys mimicked the dialogue and gesture.

"That's original," Prague huffed. "Look, can we just pretend you robosapiens got the shit kicked outta you and get on with our lives? You know that's how it's gonna go down."

The Butcher said, "You ain't got the dash, you goddamned monkey."

The Cady said something in Pentecostal tongues.

The DeVito said, "You only exist in this city becuza ME!"

The Santoro said, "That's my line," and kicked dirt on the DeVito's pants.

Prague saw that his shoelace had come loose and told his shoe to tie it. The laces threaded together into a perfect bow. He gave the Scorsese Boys a once over and hung his head. "Fine. Bring it."

The Butcher's hands metamorphosed into two giant hams. "When I close my hands," it seethed, "they become fists."

54

The Bickle ran its fingers along the ridge of a Mohawk and threw out its arm. A glinting .25 caliber sprung into its grip from inside the sleeve of its army jacket. The Santoro, DeVito and Costello followed suit. The Cady, in contrast, pulled a .44 magnum from the crotch of its chino deck pants and said, "I'm gonna make you learn about loss," in an overclocked southern drawl.

They fired.

Prague lunged into the street and somersaulted behind a parked Model T+. He clicked together the titanium rings on his thumbs and middle fingers and two Videodrome flesh-cannons burrowed out of his palms and engulfed his hands. Pushing himself off the car, he darted forward across the sidewalk, ran two steps up a brick wall, and flipped backwards...In mid-air he dodged bullets and returned the Scorsese Boys' fire, shooting them full of holes in a dizzying fit of hyperstylized Gun Kata maneuvers.

He landed on one knee with a loud boom, cracking the asphalt beneath him.

He stood.

He flexed his wrists and the Videodrome guns disappeared into his skin. Smoke hissed and oozed into the gutters.

The Scorsese Boys were badly damaged. The Costello's head had been blown in half. It lay prostrate on the hood of a Model T+, blood erupting from the wound in a seemingly endless cascade. Like all android blood, it was real...

The Bickle's coat was on fire. It tried to put it out, but the flames got larger the more it slapped them. It staggered down the street moaning and signaling taxis that weren't there. The Cady, DeVito and Santoro were veritable archery targets, their aerated bodies spurting blood. None of them expired, though, and they sized up the Anvil-in-Chief with renewed determination. So did the Butcher, who went unscathed. Prague saw to it. You don't gotta gun, you don't get the gun.

Small teams of wannabe indie filmmakers clambered out of the shadows and started jostling for footage.

Prague checked his watch. Nightly reruns of *The A-Team* began in fifteen minutes and he needed to have a shit first. Best wrap this shindig up.

The Butcher's ham-fists glistened with toxic juices that dripped onto the street in corrosive, smoking pools. Its stovepipe hat was a Leaning Tower of

Pisa that seemed on the edge of collapse. The handles of its mustache quivered. "End a the line for you, you unholy sack a shit. No sprat fucks with the Butchah. I'm an Amerikan."

"Them's fightin' words, Bill," yawned Prague. Still, the taunt worked. Prague despised the Butcher's arrogance, even if it was coded into its system. This codedness, in fact, reinforced his enmity. He had dished out Hard Goodbyes to more than ten Bill the Butcher androids in the past few years. Didn't matter how effectively. The moment its clockwork stopped ticking, a flatline signal transmitted to one of the MAP's many Culture Factories and a new Butcher was taken off a warehouse shelf like a toy in a department store.

Prague let the android get real close. He even let it give him a whack in the chops with its acidic mitts.

He grinned like a lizard as ham juice singed his cheek and mixed with martini blood. "It burns," he said...and executed one of his many token moves, the Horrorshow Splirt, a simple but devastating sleight of hand in which a Jungian psychogenetic implant allowed him to harness all of the repressed desire in his unconscious and unleash it in one mystical act of hatchetry. Contingent upon the success of the move were the retractable vibroblades implanted into the blades of his hands...

The problem with the Splirt was the imperiling fatigue that followed its execution. But Prague figured he had wounded the other Scorsese Boys sufficiently. By the time they rallied—if they rallied at all—he would be up and running again.

Reality slipped into slowtime as Prague sprung into the air, clapped his hands together, and swung down with all his strength...

The Butcher came apart like a chopped log, flying into two symmetrical halves that each exploded with purple gore. The filmmakers shouted in triumph as they devoured the imagery.

Prague collapsed.

And the DeVito and Santoro sprang to attention. Despite grave wounds, they weren't as moribund as they had let on, whereas the Cady had bled out. They bickered with each other in affected, high-pitched voices as they flipped

Prague onto his stomach, hogtied him by the wrists and ankles, and dumped him into the trunk of a postvorticist Lincoln Town Car.

In the stale darkness, Prague passed out and dreamt of a twelve-foot green monster with one brown shoe who he conjured into existence by sheer imaginative will and dexterity. At first their relationship was guarded, unsteady, and in some cases volatile. Things changed over time, and the monster evolved into an avuncular figure, teaching Prague how to do his taxes, ice fish, make beer from scratch, treat women properly, write coherent argumentative essays... One day Prague couldn't find the green monster. He searched everywhere and finally discovered it in a forest of Bonsai trees. The monster looked up at him sadly from inside the heel of its shoe. "I shrunk!" it exclaimed. "Why did you forget about me, Marshall?"

"Marshall?" said Prague, and was assaulted by a disorderly militia of men with goat heads...

Prague snorted awake as the trunk opened and the two Pesci simulacra stabbed him repeatedly with anxiety ionizers packing enough umph to mellow out a hyperactive elephant. He slipped back into dreamland...and woke up to a stainless steel rat licking his face with a dry synthetic tongue. He grabbed the rat and squeezed it until it burst in an electric plume of tinsel and clock springs.

He touched the cheek that the Bill the Butcher had punched. No scar. It had been fixed.

He had been fixed.

# 05
## Cirque de Socius

Question Mark Circus was Dr Teufelsdröckh's *cirque de preference.* Unlike the hundreds of other circuses that popped their tents within the borders of the city, he felt a sense of camaraderie here. He wasn't quite sure why—the other circuses were more or less the same jamboree with the exception of a few added scikungfi extravaganzas. Something about the place just felt like home. And the circus was a far better alternative than church or a discotheque.

Dr Teufelsdröckh purchased a small bag of caramel corn and a Shasta from an organ grinder's Grape Ape, then hunted for a seat. He wouldn't touch the caramel corn; buying it was a good faith formality he practiced whenever he attended the circus. Shasta, on the other hand, was his favorite soda. He sipped it through a straw in powerful, overjoyed bursts.

Question Mark Circus's seats had been divided into sections based on viewer identity and desire. There was a BOURGEOISIE section. There was a MEATEATERS section. There was an ESKIMOS section. There was a PLAQUEDEMICS section. There was an I ♥ ROWDY RODDY PIPER section. There was a BAD HAIRDOS and a BLACK BELTS and a THUMBTACK CONNOISSEURS and a PEOPLE WITH METASTASIZED EYEBALLS section... Failure to emulate the title of one's section of choice resulted in punishments ranging from small fines to public floggings and immolation.

Dr Teufelsdröckh selected an empty seat in the SINGLES (ENGLISH-SPEAKING) section.

...It took him nearly ten minutes to work up the nerve to talk to her. She was just his type. Big eyes. Big hairdo. Big ass. Lots of makeup. And a certain abused quality.

In the center of the ring, a nervous-looking group of lion tamers dressed in cheap tuxes waited in line to have their heads bitten off, one at a time, by a Nephilimic lion standing on its hind legs. The lion disposed of the heads in a giant brass spittoon at its side. Each lion tamer's body gushed the same blood from its neck hole.

"They're talented individuals," said the doktor, leaning towards the woman. She didn't respond. "They sure are talented." He pointed at the lion tamers.

The woman glared at him. "Did you say something?"

"Yes."

"I swear I heard somebody say something. Was it you?"

"Yes. It was me."

"I could have sworn somebody said something."

"They did. I did."

"Did you hear that? There it was again."

"I said it."

"Probably my sinuses. When they get clogged I hear all kinds of crazy shit." She looked away, massaging her nose.

The lion bit off a head and exclaimed, "That's for all you sucker MCs perpetrating a fraud," in Czech-German.

The woman clapped. "That was exciting. I wonder what he said." She turned to him. "Do you know what the lion said?"

Dr Teufelsdröckh's mouth went dry. He spoke Czech-German fluently, but he didn't know what a sucker MC was. He deflected the question with another question: "Care for some caramel corn?" He tipped the bag towards her.

She scowled at him. He smiled. She squinted at him, as if he might be standing at a distance, as if to bring his contours into focus, as if to lift the rubbery flap of his selfhood and reveal the shrieking insecurities beneath... He diverted his gaze, unable to look into any woman's eyes for more than a few seconds at a time. He had trouble looking into people's eyes in general, regardless of gender, affixing his line of vision on ears, chins, hairlines, cheekbones, background scenery, anything but the eyes...

"No thank you," she said disinterestedly. "What's your name?"

He couldn't remember...then bleated, "Dr Teufelsdröckh!" He mechanically stuck out his hand. She put her fingers in it. He squeezed the fingers and moved them up and down. He waited for her to give him her name. She didn't.

A hunchbacked Cyclops stumbled into the ring and tackled the lion. It grabbed the beast's jaws and tore it in half like a piece of cloth from mouth to anus. Then it attacked the lion tamers.

"You're a doktor?" said the woman. "What of?"

Again his memory failed him. Her breasts made him nervous. If he were to reach out and touch one of them, he might die. They were so nice-looking. So big and nice-looking..."I don't recall," he replied. "I acquired my Ph.D. long ago. But I do things. *Doktor* things. And I have a Ph.D. I procured it from Stick Figure University under the esteemed guidance of one Professor JP Timecrash. I remember that much. Are you familiar with Professor Timecrash's scholarship?"

"What's a stick figure?"

"Excuse me." A security guard placed his meathook on Dr Teufelsdröckh's shoulder. "Proof of singlehood please?"

"Yes, sir." Distressed, Dr Teufelsdröckh rifled through his pockets, the guard's long mustache brushing against his head like a dead snake.

He found the ID. He handed it to the guard.

The guard ran a fingertip over the ID and stopped on a small pink box in the lower right-hand corner. The words in the box read:

### DESPERATELY
### SEEKING SUSAN

"Thank you." The guard gave the ID back to Dr Teufelsdröckh, then leaned over and gave the woman a long, loud kiss. She complied, more or less, struggling half-heartedly. Dr Teufelsdröckh observed the kiss like a car crash on the roadside.

A flock of ironclad trapeze artists swung overhead. A flock of acrobats in winged Alligator People costumes pursued them. The trapeze artists eluded their antagonists for half a minute before pulling out cartoon Buster swords. The Alligator People impressionists countered with ray-guns. In seconds, a full-throttle wuxia pan battle royal erupted...

The woman dabbed her lips with a napkin. "Strangers take advantage of me."

A clump of burnt flesh landed on Dr Teufelsdröckh's knee. He slapped it off. "They do?" He didn't know what else to say to her. The security guard derailed his nerves. Authority figures always had that effekt. "That seems normal enough, I suppose."

Stand up and leave, he told himself. Get up. *Sofort.* Do it....But he couldn't do it. He tried to place his thoughts elsewhere, to breathe in and out, to anaesthetize his mental core, to think about food, the perfect gourmet meal, a utopian spread, a French spread, herb pâté for an appetizer, a frisée salad with goat cheese and balsamic syrup, a main course of *Épaule d'agneau aux anchois*, and for dessert, hmm, what the hell would he eat for dessert?...

Her gaze moved up and down his body and settled on his lower region. Was she staring at his love handles? Couldn't be. He was wearing a Blubsucker. He had only bought the shirt last week, an anti-love handle apparatus that constricted flab at the waist and redistributed it to the groin. Was the shirt defective? Did he still have the receipt? If not, would the department store from which he purchased the shirt refund his money? Would the store refund his money in any case?

"I'm building a monster!" he blurted, eyeballing a freak in a spiked cage. Outside the cage, a clown with a spear stabbed at the freak and forced it to impale itself on the spikes, which faced inwards.

"What's a monster?" She put her hand on his leg.

His heart skipped a beat. "What's a monster?" He contemplated the question as the freak hemorrhaged impossible quantities of celluloid from multiple wounds...He said: "The OED describes a monster as a mythical creature that exhibits both animal and human qualities or combines elements of one or more animal forms. Frequently this creature is of great size and ferocious appearance. That's an antiquated notion, however. Contemporary perspectives of the monster reveal an imaginary creature that may be large, ugly, or frightening. For the record, my monster won't be *large*, per se. It will, however, be equipped with the capacity to transform into a *daikaiju*."

"What's a OED? What's a ferocious appearance? What's a contemporary perspectives? What's a *dai...dai...?*" She moved her hand up his thigh. Cries of agony overhead, below, everywhere...

As each sentence exited his mouth, he sat up straighter in his seat, gaining confidence, becoming more passionate and electric. He was in his element now. "It will appear human. All too human. It will be a crossbreed. A *Mischling,* if you please. Nobody has done it before. Monsters have been made, no doubt, but not of this caliber. Certainly not of this imaginative *Größe*. I will give the world what it needs, what it desires. What it despises. And when the sun sets on humanity, people will glance over their shoulders on the long walk to oblivion and say, 'Teufelsdröckh!' Nothing can stop me. The future is now. The future is *me*. I am going to splice together the personages of Adolph Hitler and John Keats!"

He leapt out of his seat as he cried out.

The singles behind him shouted obscenities, complaining that his love handles were blocking their view. He sat back down.

The woman said, "My name's Delilah Jive," as if Dr Teufelsdröckh had just sat down next to her for the first time. He ignored the introduction. He had slipped into a dimension of sheer subjectivity and egoism. All he could hear, all he could speak was the Dialogue of the Self. "One might ask why I elect these figures. Allow me a small degree of persiflage. The choice of Hitler seems obvious enough: despite a healthy assortment of raw, evil-spirited shortcomings, the Führer was a genius. He merely lacked the capacity to flourish as an *artiste*. He wanted to be a painter, you see. But he wasn't very good at painting, and everybody told him so. Sublimation resulted. He redirected the flows of his desire into politics, a realm in which he excelled, albeit through a proverbial glass darkly. Hence the transformation of a Fuck All You Bastards sentiment into an art form, namely in the shape of genocide, world domination, public speaking, and funny-looking modes of walking forward *en masse*, i.e., the goose-step. Moral: don't asphyxiate a would-be creative mind, however competent or inadequate. At any rate, John Keats is a less likely candidate, perhaps. He died before his time at the age of twenty-five in 1821. Tuberculosis, of course. His artistry emerged in the form of poems. Epics the likes of 'Hyperion,' 'Endymion' and 'The Eve of St Agnes' are the most widely regarded crowdpleasers, as are the various odes, namely 'Grecian Urn,' 'Nightingale,' 'Psyche' and 'Melancholy.' Personally I prefer the boy's shorter pieces 'La Belle Dame sans Merci' and 'I stood tip-toe upon a little hill,' but I have a relatively short attention span, and that's my problem. What intrigues me most about Keats is his theory of negative capability, which essentially posits that a man can take comfort in human uncertainties and the inaccessible nature of reality if only that man puts his mind to it. In this fashion, then, Keats deploys a potentially crippling pessimism as a springboard for a terrifically powerful optimism that echoes across hills and valleys. Here's the rub: unlike Hitler, Keats was a successful *artiste*. He had many contemporary critics, but today his work is perceived as among the finest in the corpus of British literature. I believe John Keats will provide me with the imaginative and stylistic mettle I need to create an Adolph Hitler of epidemic proportions. I will, in short, inject Hitler with Keats and thus render him the *artiste* he never was and always wanted to be. And, of course, I will sprinkle a pinch of *daikaiju* on the finished product. Through the vehicle of this Portrait of an *Artiste* as a Young Man, I will distinguish myself as an *artiste* myself. The ultimate *artiste*. An *artiste* for the end of the world! End exposition."

War broke out. Scikungfi masters invaded the tent like a flock of vampire bats, attacking circus performers and circus-goers with equal intensity, flying back and forth as if on wires, ripping off body parts, swinging and twirling staffs and nunchucks and electric eels and hurling endless splash weapons that mangled their targets irreconcilably. Whips cracked. Jungle cats roared. An out-of-place flapper sang earsplitting doo-wop...Stench of manure. Hay bales on fire...Genetically enhanced porcupines fired mushroom clouds of poisonous quills that made people explode. Jugglers threw torches at hot dog salesmen. Tightrope walkers hung themselves with bungee nooses. An electric mastodon with a preprogrammed prejudice against birdwatchers stomped on one, two, three, four birdwatchers...Tsunami of surrogate blood, mudslide of entrails. Haunted house screeches and moans...Pulp alien octopi-craft stormed the circus, reducing animals, humans, mutants to puddles of semi-conscious sludge. A brigade of comic book superheroes followed in the aliens' train and committed their own irreplaceable acts of ultraviolence...

...*Cirque de socius*, thought Dr Teufelsdröckh. If a man doesn't have a woman, he tries to get a woman. If a man has a woman, he tries to get another woman. *Fin*...

He opened an umbrella to shield himself from the rain of gore. "I have in my possession one of John Keats' death masks," he continued, oblivious, raising his voice above the hullabaloo. "It's an original, constructed the day after he died by a Roman *creatore del candlestick*. Do you know that Keats' visage was the spitting image of Jean-Claude Van Damme's? The cheekbones. The lips. The chin...Do you know who Jean-Claude Van Damme was? Have you ever seen the film *Bloodsport*? Let me ask you this: have you ever seen *No Retreat, No Surrender*, or, even better, *Breakin'*? Van Damme appeared in all of these films. And while his acting skills left something to be desired, he certainly did have a nice body, and he was a remarkable protoscikungfi fighter. If only Keats had possessed the actor's body. And his moves."

Dr Teufelsdröckh ventured a look at Delilah Jive. She was dead. And in two parts. One part twitched wildly on the floor as the other leaked aromatic coffee beans.

How long had he been talking to himself?

He felt a tug on his shoulder. He turned around.

Truth.

"What the? How did you get in here?"

Truth shrugged. "Beauty ate all the celery. We need more." He shrugged again. "What should I do?"

Poltergeists began to leap out of people and devour the residual bodies. "Christ. I can't leave you alone for fifteen minutes." It was time to leave anyway. But that didn't mean Dr Teufelsdröckh had to like it. He tried to steady his breath, wondering what Truth and Beauty could have been doing with celery. He despised celery. An entirely lackluster vegetable. He certainly wouldn't have authorized its use, even privately. "This is the last straw," he assured Truth. "Come with me."

Escorted by the gongs of Apocalypse, the doktor and his assistant left the Question Mark Circus, tipping the head waiter at the door as they hurried into the brown night.

# 06
## The Count of Vincent Prague

"Eighty-six, eighty-seven, eighty-eight, eighty-nine, nrrrrrrr..."

He trailed off. He hadn't been counting long. But there was nothing else to do. He grew bored of the count quicker than desired or anticipated. How long had he been incarcerated here? No more than a few hours. Maybe just a few minutes. Now what could he do?

This is what happened next: eighteen years passed...

# 07
# Eleven Mad Scientists & Fifty-Five Monsters

The monster-making kit came with four additional items, free of charge: a Mr Hyde action figure, a test tube of hemlock (in case the final product turned against its master), a vintage 8-track cassette tape of the Cryptkicker's song "Monster Mash" (incl. four remixes), and a lock of Mary Shelley's hair. The hair wasn't authentic, but it had been cloned from a simulacrum of a replica of a carbon copy of a genetic twin of the original mane's imagined DNA. Batteries not included.

"For a little extra," said the monster peddler, "I'll throw in this DAT, too. Can't get this one anywhere anymore." He inserted the tape into a vaginal slit that opened in his forehead, pressed his right nipple, and opened his mouth. A Bass-O-Matic version of "The Purple People Eater" flooded the room.

"No thank you!"

He pressed his left nipple, closed his mouth. "Suit yourself. Your loss." His chest ejected the tape. The monster peddler crushed it in his fist and tossed it into an incinerator hole. "Everything's in the contract," he grumbled, "although this is the black market and contracts are entirely irrelevant and worthless. But I like to tickle my customer's funny bones."

"Ha ha ha ha ha ha ha."

"That was a fake laugh. Just remember what I told you about making the unit your own. Basic assembly is only the first step. After that, it's up to you. Your monster can be anything you want it to be as long as you don't muck it up. Get it?"

"I understand."

"I require a signature at this point please."

"Signature? I thought this was the black market?"

The monster peddler pointed at his elbow. "Funny bone." He handed the customer a slip of paper and a magic marker. "At the bottom, sir, please."

Dr Teufelsdröckh perused the document:

**QUANTITY 1 ACME MONSTER MAKING KIT® sold to QUANTITY 1 PERSON. The seller is not responsible for ANYTHING that happens (pertaining to the aforementioned ACME MONSTER MAKING KIT® or life and the universe in general) after the conclusion of this transaction to QUANTITY 1 PERSON, who buys at his own risk, of his own free will, and according to his own code of ethics.**

Satisfied, he put his signature on the document—

## Honk Honk!

—and removed his spectacles. The monster peddler scanned his retinas and extracted payment.

"You know, those sight refining instruments are out of style." The monster peddler pointed at the spectacles.

"Sight refining instruments? You mean my glasses?"

"Glasses? I drink from glasses, sir. I don't look through them."

Dr Teufelsdröckh put his spectacles back on. "*Auf Wiedersehen.*" Tucking the box in an armpit, he crawled out of the manhole and rolled across the street onto a slidewalk...

That evening, in the laboratory...

"It isn't working!" exclaimed Truth. Beauty cowered behind an anatomical skeleton as the monster repeatedly stabbed itself with shards of broken test tubes. They had already made ten monsters. None of them worked. That is, all of them either failed to come to life or came to life and tried to commit suicide. The assistants began to spin Grimm-like fairy tales in which ne'er a monster functioned properly.

Dr Teufelsdröckh remained positive. "Chins up. Panic theories are for the Henpecked." He struck the monster in the back of the head with a hammer. A bolt of wet lightning exited the wound and the monster collapsed. Truth and Beauty took it by the arms and legs and heaved it atop the pile of monsters in the corner. "What we need," the doctor said, "is an effektive architect. Clearly I am not that architect. But perhaps I can create an organism capable of creating my *desiratum*."

"Perhaps," said Truth, overconfident in the doktor's power to fail.

...The subsequent *Wütendeswissenschaftlermunster* (trans. mad scientist monster) was eight feet tall.

Truth and Beauty tried to strap a lab jacket onto the *Wütendeswissenschaftlermunster* that was six sizes too small. The *Wütendeswissenschaftlermunster* swatted them away. But the assistants kept coming back. Eventually Dr Teufelsdröckh blew its head off with a shotgun. "Too tall," he noted.

The next *Wütendeswissenschaftlermunster* was not only too short, it had a severe case of phocomelia; armless, its hands hung from its shoulders like rubber gloves. Dr Teufelsdröckh plunged a *nagamaki* into its chest...

The third *Wütendeswissenschaftlermunster* looked like Donald Pleasence.

"Donald Pleasence?" said Beauty, raising his bushy eyebrow. Juxtaposed with its considerably diminished peer, the eyebrow looked alive. As if, the doktor thought, it might be an organism in and of itself.

"He played Dr Loomis in those *Halloween* movies," said Dr Teufelsdröckh. "Sam Loomis?"

Truth shook his head.

"You've never heard of a movie called *Halloween*? Or *Halloween II*? And so on? I should fire you for that alone."

"I only watch silent films," said Beauty.

"I saw *Halloween III: Season of the Witch*," bragged Truth.

"I wasn't in that installment," admitted the *Wütendeswissenschaftlermunster* in an aggrieved British accent. "Nor was Michael Myers. *Season of the Witch* has nothing to do with the *Halloween* series. The plot concerns an

evil-doing corporate magnate who manufactures a line of novelty masks that
spew serpents and ooze bugs and eat people's heads. Brilliant. But an anomaly.
A barracuda in an aardvark colony, so to speak. And yet I'd argue that it's easily
the best installment."

"I can't disagree," said the doktor, and killed the *Wütendeswissenschaftlermunster* with a geyser gun...

The eighth *Wütendeswissenschaftlermunster* finally satisfied the doktor,
but after failing to create eleven functioning monsters, he killed it and created
another one, which failed to create twelve functioning monsters before
losing its life. He told the tenth *Wütendeswissenschaftlermunster* to create
another *Wütendeswissenschaftlermunster* to do the job that neither it nor
its colleagues hadn't been able to do. The *Wütendeswissenschaftlermunster*
resisted, claiming it wasn't like the others. It also claimed that it was a
deeply spiritual being and a son of God and killing it would be murder. Dr
Teufelsdröckh thought: What would Thomas Carlyle do in his position? Give
the *Wütendeswissenschaftlermunster* the benefit of the doubt? Respect
its spirit of faith in God and itself? Dr Teufelsdröckh tried to embrace an
Everlasting Yea...which, per usual, was usurped by an Everlasting No,
and he insisted that the *Wütendeswissenschaftlermunster* create another
*Wütendeswissenschaftlermunster* to do his bidding. Reluctantly the *Wütendeswissenschaftlermunster* obeyed...and created another Donald Pleasence
lookalike. This one, however, possessed venomous tentacles and a deadly
mouth-within-a-mouth à la the *Alien* film franchise.

"That's better than I could do," the doktor admitted. "But not good enough."

He ordered the Pleasence/Alien *Wütendeswissenschaftlermunster* to kill its
maker, then itself. The monster croaked, "Nothing can stop Michael Myers..."

..."I don't understand it." Dr Teufelsdröckh poured himself a glass of table
wine and took a sip. He cut up a block of Gruyere cheese and ate a slice. He
chased the Gruyere with a croissant. Truth and Beauty watched him. "There.
That's better." He wiped off his mouth. "What am I doing wrong? I followed
the instructions."

"Sometimes instructions lie," said Truth.

"Instructions don't lie," replied the doktor. "Truth lies."

"Him, you mean?" asked Beauty, pointing at Truth. "Or the concept of honesty?"

Truth punched Beauty.

"*Hören Sie auf!*" Dr Teufelsdröckh finished the wine and put his glass aside. "At any rate, these *Wütendeswissenschaftlermunsters* are a waste of time, energy and resources. If one wants something done, one must do the thing oneself."

Twenty-two monsters later...

"That looks like Jean-Claude Van Damme with a mustache," admitted Truth, itching an armpit. The burlap fabric of his orderly uniform was almost unbearable. But the doktor insisted, advocating burlap's many half-lives.

"I disagree," said Beauty. "Dressed in a bowler hat and tramp suit, it would bear an unmistakable likeness to Charlie Chaplin."

Truth huffed. "You're wrong. Its face is too sharp and angular."

The monster goosestepped back and forth across the laboratory, reciting fragments of "Endymion." Now and then it tripped over discarded body parts and slipped on puddles of viscera, motor oil and fiberoptics, but it never fell down. Dr Teufelsdröckh looked at the monster with equal measures of terror and wonderment.

Truth said, "It's not as ripped up as Van Damme, though. Van Damme had a better body. He was like an anatomical dummy. He was probably a clockwork man. This thing is downright flabby by comparison."

"*Anschlag!*"

The monster froze. Dr Teufelsdröckh tentatively approached it.

He touched its shoulder. He tugged on its genitals. He ran a finger over the flesh of its abdomen. Finally he stabbed it in the navel with a turkey baster and squeezed the bulb...

The monster simmered, boiled...inflated. Its body erupted with muscle and its skin contracted against the muscle as if pulled taught by a drawstring. The final product was a hyperreal caricature of an anabolically enhanced human body that bore resemblance to an animatronic cartoon.

"I stand corrected," said Truth, itching his thighs, his knees. "This outfit is an atrocity."

"Wear it!" shouted Dr Teufelsdröckh.

"Why are women who have miscarriages always *whisked* away?" wondered Beauty. "They're never rolled away, or carried away, or wheelbarrowed away. They're always *whisked*."

Truth snarled, "That doesn't have anything to do with anything. Wake up."

"I'm awake." He thought about the assertion. "I'm pretty sure I'm awake. I can't be certain. This may be the nightmare of reality."

Truth attacked him.

Dr Teufelsdröckh stroked the monster's mustache. "Keats stands to profit by this manner of vivisection. Rumor was he had difficulty growing facial hair. Wordsworth wrote a long poem about it that was originally intended to be part of his *Prelude*, but Coleridge allegedly ate the manuscript one night in a doped up frenzy. This was when Wordsworth was living with his sister Dorothy at Dove Cottage in the Lake District. On the night in question, Dorothy tried to kick the author of 'Kubla Khan' out, but he rebuffed her, and he flew into a rage, and in addition to trashing the cottage and eating 'Book XV: The Unbearded Nancy Boy,' as it was called, he bit the head off of the Wordsworth's canary and set fire to the dining room. Coleridge was a madman. But Wordsworth endured him. The point is, Keats couldn't grow so much as a sideburn, and everybody made fun of him for it. Now look at him." He stroked the mustache with increasing excitement. The monster frowned. Behind them, Truth and Beauty crashed and rolled through the carnage. "On another note, where would aesthetics be today in the absence of Adolph Hitler and the Nazi holocaust? Think of all the art that has been produced as a direct corollary to World War II-related hatemongering. Cinema, literature, music. Digigraffiti. Architecture. Countless artifacts of text and image. I believe the root cause of World War II was not German Aryanism but an entropic deprivation of the artistic spirit in the human condition on a global scale. There can be no art in the absence of evil deeds, after all. An artist can't subsist on smiles and handshakes. The Giant Ogre of Cruelty and Violence must bear its screaming asshole to the world in order for an artist to sufficiently realize his talents. World War II was simply an instance of humanity giving itself a venue for future creative expression during a period of dangerous imaginative stasis." The monster sneezed. Dr Teufelsdröckh began to stroke his own overlip. His assistants' horseplay continued without remittance. "That reminds me," he continued, "I still need to download and print out a thimble of *daikaiju* DNA. Where's the computer? Where's the prototyper? Look at this godforsaken zoo…"

# 08
## Houses of If

It was a simulacrum of Edmond Dantès' cell in the island prison Château d'If in Alexandre Dumas' French adventure novel *The Count of Monte Cristo*. Prague knew because of the inscription on the stone wall. Which read: THIS IS A SIMULACRUM OF EDMOND DANTÈS' CELL IN THE ISLAND PRISON CHÂTEAU D'IF IN ALEXANDRE DUMAS' FRENCH ADVENTURE NOVEL *THE COUNT OF MONTE CRISTO.*

He ran a fingertip over the words. "If..."

The first year was the hardest. It took a long time to relegate the pangs of hunger, physically and psychologically; he had always possessed a vicious appetite and a speedy metabolism to keep him nice and trim. A rusty metal slot in the cell door opened three times a day and somebody tossed in a tin plate of goulash or soup or gruel. Bad things ensued. He was accustomed to overeating and his body took revenge by way of frequent diarrhea, nausea, hives, cold shakes, brainfreeze, and other unpleasant symptoms of excess-deprived withdrawal. Additionally, a man in an iron blowtorch mask tortured him on a regular basis. The man never used a blowtorch. He used a magnifying glass, burning holes in Prague's skin with the aid of a portable fusion-powered sun, but usually the man beat him with blunt, Lo-Tech weapons (e.g. clubs, maces, logs, chains, pipes, baseball bats, bones, candlesticks, broomsticks, hardcover books, stones, bricks, icicles, chair legs, medicine balls, T-squares, hippopotamus whips, shower nozzles, flashlights, knobkieries, sally rods, wrenches, bamboo, etc.). He only tortured Prague once with surgical instruments, cutting off most of his fingers and toes as well as a pound of flesh here and there and the majority of his upper lip. Whatever the case, Prague oscillated between screaming, giggling and snoring, unable to retaliate given the steady influx of sleeping and laughing gases into his cell.

After awhile, Prague adapted to the routine. Even defecating in a bucket wasn't unbearable. Nor was having his veins artlessly replenished with fresh Victory gin and vermouth whenever it went bad. His only real complaint was the constant draft he felt on his upper row of teeth; he realized the grave degree to which he had taken his lip for granted. He even befriended his torturer, who, while continuing to bruise, burn and break him, developed a high regard for the celebrity/g-man/prisoner, telling him jokes and, once, bringing him a slice of cherry pie.

One day the torturer entered the cell and began to cry. Prague asked him why. He took off his blowtorch mask, revealing the surgically reconstructed face of Vincent Prague *sans défaut*, and said, "Seven years have passed. That's seven tenths of a decade." He fell to his knees, sobbing.

Behind the torturer appeared a replica of Armand Dorleac, the prison warden of Château d'If in an early twentieth century film version of *The Count of Monte Cristo*. He placed a hand on the torturer's shoulder. "Pardon the poor fool. Upon your incarceration, he had his face recreated in your image and has become quite attached to you, I'm afraid. Now we'll have to burn the visage to ashes. Alas."

Prague lifted a trembling arm and pointed at the warden. "You look familiar. Didn't you play bad guys in *Robin Hood: Prince of Thieves* and *The Crow*? *Strange Days*, I think, too."

"Amazing, Mr Prague," said the warden. "How do you speak so well in the absence of your upper lip? Bilabials are an impossible feat of articulation in your condition."

"Ventriloquism runs in my family."

"Ah yes. Of course. What doesn't run in your family? Well, you're free to go. You've paid your debt."

"Debt? Fuck did I do?"

"You know the MAP. Existence itself is grounds for punishment. Thus and so. By the way may I have your autograph? My kids love your work." He held out a sheet of parchment paper and a fountain pen.

Prague took the pen and threw it aside. He blew his nose onto the paper and gave it back to the warden.

Bound in shackles at the neck, wrists and ankles, he shuffled up and down and across countless stairways and corridors and planks, pausing only to be flogged by malicious escorts...

A doktor stood at the front gate of Château d'If. He wore a stethoscope and monocle and pale green OR uniform. "Hmm," he said at the sight of Prague, and took his pulse. "I see. Take him to the madhouse, please. This man is insane in the membrane."

"Insane in the brain," droned the diminutive assistant at the doktor's side.

An escort clubbed Prague in the back of the head. Before losing consciousness, he felt somebody tear another chunk from his thigh.

Next: Another seven years elapsed...

Prague awoke in a straightjacket and muzzle gag. His cell looked roughly the same size as the one in Château d'If. It was much taller, though, and the walls were padded. And instead of an inscription that read THIS IS A SIMULACRUM OF EDMOND DANTÈS' CELL IN THE ISLAND PRISON CHÂTEAU D'IF IN ALEXANDRE DUMAS' FRENCH ADVENTURE NOVEL *THE COUNT OF MONTE CRISTO*, there was a flickering neon sign that read KILROY WAS HERE. In the background, rock opera band Styx's song "Mr Roboto" played over and over and over. Prague hung from the ceiling, upside-down, by a long copper wire...

"We want you to get better," said hospital director Doktor Ray B Flechsig on Day 1 through a yellow, bearded grin.

"What's wrong with me?" wheezed Prague.

Flechsig punched him in the balls. "Your nuts hurt, for one. But that's neither here nor there. Nurse?"

A bleached blond wearing a peephole leather bra, fishnet stockings and fishbowl pumps appeared at Flechsig's side. The doktor pointed at Prague's crotch. Smiling, the nurse stomped on his crotch with her heels and reduced his genitals to stir-fry.

By Day 563, Prague felt settled in. He had gotten used to hanging upside down, more or less, envisioning himself as an elderly bat who just wanted to stay in his cave, and "Mr Roboto" no longer ailed him; he had exorcized the song of all clandestine messages, references and innuendo. He could barely hear the song, even though half a year ago somebody turned the volume on full blast.

Six times a day, Doktor Flechsig sent in the nurse to feed and sedate him. She removed his muzzle gag, shoved a spoonful of goo into his mouth, and chased the goo with a pill. Sometimes she cradled his head and emptied a shot of shitty scotch into his throat. Sometimes she clutched his hair and kissed him. Her lips felt like tarantula legs. Her tongue felt like leather.

On Day 1,241, they cut Prague down and unleashed him into the general population. It took 100+ days to get used to standing and walking upright.

Patients weren't allowed to wear clothes. Orderlies shaved them from head to toe with dull straight razors every day. A mechanical pharmacist stalked them constantly, machinegunning pills that were absorbed into the skin on impact. Patients had to sleep two per single cot. Prague's bedmate was a cannibal. Every morning he woke up bleeding martini juice, chunks of flesh torn from his limbs, abdomen and back, and he had to visit the medical ward, which was owned and operated by cannibal sympathizers who reluctantly sewed Prague up, although not without serving him a fair share of pro-cannibal propaganda. Soon the hospital ran out of Victory gin and vermouth and they filled Prague's veins with cow spit. At this point he truly went insane. He believed he was a robot. He walked like a robot. He talked like a robot. He made robotic gestures and signals and tics. Then he recovered. He slept, dreaming again and again of the Nowhere Man. One night Doktor Flechsig shook him awake. "I love you," he said, and molested Prague.

500+ days later, a man draped in a bed sheet served the Anvil-in-Chief walking papers.

Prague had been eaten so badly over the years he looked more like a turkey bone than a human being. The twilight zone of modern science and technology permitted him to function, however, as did the power of ventriloquism, his bedmate having devoured his lower lip and equipped him with a permanent rictus grin.

This state of extreme deformity excited Doktor Flechsig. He hugged Prague tightly on his way out of the ward, rubbing genitals against his leg, whispering, "I never want to let go." But he did let go. And it wasn't until Prague skulked down an interminable hallway into an elevator that he encountered further difficulty.

"What floor, sir?" said an aged elevator operator.

"The one with the cafeteria."

"Certainly." The doors closed and the elevator went down. "Say, don't I know you? I think you were in a bad dream I had last night."

"Boo."

He pushed the emergency stop button and faced Prague. "Seriously. Haven't I seen you somewhere before? Sir, I think I've seen you."

Prague lost his cool and tried to strangle the elevator operator. Years of sedation and loss of flesh rendered him pitiably weak and forlorn, and the incensed elevator operator, who may have been in his early 90s, manhandled him like a scarecrow, slamming him against the walls and then kneeing him in the groin. Prague crumpled. The elevator operator kicked him until the elevator sighed to a stop, the bell went ding, and the doors slid open.

The police awaited him.

The next four years transpired in a semi-conscious blur as Prague was transported from clink to clink...They beat him with billy clubs for three weeks, working in shifts. They pinned him to a wall and threw ripe bananas at him for over a month. They cooked him for thirty seconds at a time in a walk-in microwave oven. They snipped off the rest of his fingers and toes. They starved him, fed him, starved him. They sequestered halfass dentists to enact Knievelesque surgical procedures, sans anesthesia, on his molars. They threw him into a pool of cybernetic leeches and dared him to swim out. They castrated him. They boiled him. They plucked him. They opened a door and told him to go. Prague slumped towards freedom. They slammed shut the door just before he reached it and kicked the shit out of him. They performed this routine 120,346 times...They locked him in a House of Usher haunted by belligerent Edgar

Allen Poe ghosts. The ghosts leapt into Prague's body, engaging it in precarious sexual acts and forcing it to sign incalculable quantities of autographs. Prague moaned. He shrieked. He gurgled and vomited and passed out and dreamt and awoke and growled and croaked and cramped and exploded with rage and enmity and imploded with fear and apathy and went delirious from the pain the pain THE PAIN...They locked him in a mausoleum constructed entirely out of telescreens (walls, ceilings, floors, sarcophagi) that broadcast footage of Vincent Prague's former public arrests, car chases, scikungfi fights, barista beatings, snake charmings, stand-up routines, assassinations, etc. At this point Prague was a mere quivering lump of flesh that could have easily been mistaken for a pile of elephant shit with a hairdo. But he was alive. They made certain to keep him on the razor's edge of Life at all times.

At last a farmhand entered the mausoleum, shoveled Prague into a wheelbarrow and ferried him outside. Sunlight stung his exposed eyeballs. Welcome pain. Another week of self-infested screenlight would have cooked him to the bone...

...solarized flashbulbs of agony as they poured his body into a re-animator drum and sang:

> *Oh Mr Johnny Verbeck how could you be so mean?*
> *I told you you'd be sorry for inventing that machine.*
> *Now all the neighbors cats and dogs will never more be seen.*
> *They'll all be ground to sausages in Johnny Verbeck's machine. Hey!*

But by the time they had finished the last chorus, he had regained his body, lock, stock and barrel, without a scratch, although he was almost two decades older now, and the Victory martini they siphoned into his veins contained too much olive juice...

"Good morning, Mr Prague," said a maître d'. "Observe, if you will, the mechanism. She's Wellsian through and through. This glittering metallic framework is a state-of-the-art apparatus. Its singularly askew transparent crystalline substance commands the attention of any passerby with half a defragmented brain. Note the mechanism's twinkling, brilliantly illuminated appearance. Need I mention the ivory fixtures? The brass candlesticks are certainly a nice touch, too, wouldn't you say? All for the reasonable price of $9,999.99. That's for one ride. That includes a bag of popcorn, I might add. Portions of soda start at $800 per Dixie cup."

Prague paid with a thumbprint, climbed into the saddle of the time machine, and put on his seat belt.

Half a minute later he stood in Commodore Rabelais's office.

"Welcome back, Mr Anvil-in-Chief." Rabelais scraped his incisor with a toothpick. "I say that to your conscious as much as to your corporeal self. The year is Ticky Tacky 8.4. I just spoke to you three hours ago. You just spoke to me eighteen years and three hours ago. Here." He slid a box of cigarettes across the desk. "Smoke these. Each cigarette will return to your body one year of its life, plus two additional years, if you elect to smoke the entire pack. Time, time, time—have you seen what's become of you? You're a wrinkled mess. You're fit for the grave. And you're only fifty-one years old, technically speaking. I'd guess you were ninety-one, if I looked at you askance. But I rarely look at people askance." He flicked the toothpick across the office. A mechanical hand reached out of a trash can and claimed it before it struck the floor. "We may want to do something about your memory, though. Torture isn't a pleasant thing to reflect on, particularly that which has been enacted by your loving employer. Another pack of cigarettes will take care of any mnemonic turbulence. Well. On behalf of the MAP, I assure you this little diversion has all been proffered in the name of character development. I hope you've learned your lesson and are ready and willing to do your duty."

Prague opened the cigarette box, took one out and lit it. He inhaled deeply and swallowed the smoke.

# 09
## Untitled Teufelsdröckh Rejektion Letter (on Cooking Channel Letterhead)

1 January 10,023 AR[1]

Dr Hermann Teufelsdröckh, Ph.D.
1-2X Das Schloß
Kount Westwest Prachtstraße
843 227853 Prague
Former Czech Republik

Dear Dr Teufelsdröckh:

Thank you for your recent submission to The Cooking Channel for the position of Associate Celebrity of Gourmevangelism®. We received your varied follow-up letters and apologize for the delayed response. A six year turnaround, however, is not an unreasonable stretch of time considering the vast number of

---

1    An abbreviation that, according to *The Encyclopedia of Johnny Mnemonics*, simultaneously denotes "After Reality" and "Alpha Ricardo." This revision of the temporal calendar from the former AD (Anno Domini) commenced the year after the death of Mexican-born actor Ricardo Montalbán, who, after being resuscitated from his first death in 2009, lived to be 312 years old and for most of his life was widely perceived as a messiah and an enthusiastic violator of the laws of reality. Despite his eventual final death at the hands of an extremist cult of Urban-Amerikan Bushman, the star of renowned television series *Fantasy Island* (1978-84; 2030-39; 2167-2232) maintained a firm grip on the collective consciousness and incited new ways of perceiving the human condition and achieving new metaphysical heights.

submissions we receive on a daily basis. At any rate, we thank you for your patience and hope to find you in good health.

While we enjoyed your video footage, we regret to inform you that we have decided to pass on your candidacy as host of our upcoming show, *Chuka Ichiban Inframan*, which will debut on 22 March 10,025 AR. Don't forget to tune in! We would also like to take this opportunity to discourage you from further submissions. Rest assured, we will keep your footage on file in the event that a suitable TCC Irreality TV venue comes to fruition. We understand how difficult this must be for you. We recommend comfort food the likes of which you might find on virtually every one of our shows, including reruns, spoofs, spinoffs and hypermelodramatizations.

"The mass of men lead lives of quixotic douchebaggery." Are you familiar with this timeless apothegm? We hope it might give you some degree of solace in your time of need and perdition. We apologize for this impersonal form letter. If you require further service, please contact us at our head office in Prague. Bear in mind, we do not possess hard communications technology of any kind, or, if we do, we are unauthorized to inform you as to its numeric and linguistic stature. If you wish to contact us, you must do so in person. The waiting room is in the basement.

In the meantime, we leave you with the following story, which, alongside the aforementioned apothegm, is intended to lift your spirits: There was a man who kept a manhole, and he enjoyed the manhole as much as he enjoyed the sun, wary of their differences and eccentricities. One morning he lost the capacity to tell the difference between the two circular-shaped articles. He suspected the sun had been a manhole all along. Troubled, he ate breakfast without the assistance of utensils...and suddenly everything fell into place. The man put on sunglasses, crawled into the sun and went to sleep. And the manhole closed like a bank vault.

The end.

Sincerely,

*Jav*

Mr Javier Flankeater, Chef-in-Chief
The Cooking Channel
c/o Stick Figure Incorporated
c/o/o MAP Home-Ek Department
1145 Gud Food Street
City City, State 83
USAmerika

# 10
## Tranzatlanticism

Vincent Prague placed a razor on his cheek and considered the prospect of being a hole. A black hole.

"Is there any other kind?" said a voice in his head.

He entertained a mental soliloquy on the nature of holes. How they provide access. How they function as entryways and exits. One can vanish into a hole. One can crawl out of it, or stay inside. Bodies are made of holes (i.e. pores). Bodies come from holes (i.e. vaginas) and return to holes (i.e. graves). The earth is full of holes (i.e. gorges, basins, canyons, chasms, ravines, etc.). The universe itself is full of holes, howling gaps of nothingness carved into the empty fabric of space, time and psyche. The universe, as a matter of fact, is one great hole. And we're all inside of it. Any desire to be a hole is rendered null and void by dint of this cold, hard reality (i.e. I am already a hole). The question, then, is not: To be or not to be a hole? The question is: Have I ever been anything but a hole? No, that's not the question. The question is: To what degree am I a hole (i.e. what is the severity or paucity of my holehood, i.e., my hole-*I*-ness)?

The vidphone rang. He shaved his face in six broad strokes. The vidphone hung up and rang again. He listened to it. It hung up and rang again four more times.

He went into the kitchen and touched a miniscreen. "I am a hole where something else used to be," he said.

"Grow up, wiseass," said the visage of Foghorn Leghorn in a thick Southern drawl. "Quit piddling, I say. Get down here now, boy. Pronto. I say, I do say now, we're waiting for you at Slingpad 7-2521 on Rooftop 1984 of MAP Spacescraper D-503. Look here."

Prague thought Yosemite Sam would be a more adequate representation of Administrator Wichita's persona than Foghorn Leghorn. Was the vidphone on the fritz? Then again, he didn't know the director that well. His only sustained interaction with him had been a pep talk he received before the now legendary scikungfi fight with the Nowhere Man; otherwise he had only communicated with Wichita over the vidphone. And yet Prague possessed an almost extraterrestrial ability to read people. It only took a few interlocutions for him to determine if somebody was an asshole or not so much of an asshole—the only two possible states of existence for a human being and most simulacra.

"I know where you're waiting for me," replied Prague. "I'll be there in twenty minutes."

He showed up at Slingpad 7-2521 three days later.

A long line of wilburies spiraled around the slingatron as bodies fell out of the sky into colossal pillows. Sometimes they missed the pillows and splattered against the concrete like bugs on a windshield. Misfired arrivals with sufficient funds were IDed, scraped up, and ushered into reanimation booths. Plebs, proles and other non-Fredersons were squeegeed into gutter holes.

Multicolored spotlights illuminated the slingpad in a hot frenzy. An orchestra of Victorian mannequins played Black Lodge melodia. Tall, beetlelike sentinels fished new arrivals out of the landing pillows and ushered them into glitzy Duty Free shops. Anyone who resisted or refused a shopping spree was arrested or executed on the spot.

Flanked by two SAMSAs, Administrator Wichita gesticulated wildly. "Vincent Prague!" he exclaimed, delirious with fatigue and angst.

"That's Mr Anvil-in-Chief to you." For no particular reason, Prague roundhoused one of the SAMSAs with maximum force, cracking his neck. An arthropodal leg burst from his suit coat like a clock spring and the SAMSA collapsed. The other SAMSA hoisted the body over a shoulder and carried him away. "Nice work, fellas," said Prague, putting down his briefcase. He eyed Wichita. "That's what I call efficiency. Guess you'll have to put my seatbelt on."

"Come back here! Goddamn functionaries. They get more schized every day." Wichita prodded Prague with a finger. "General Assistant Managerial Choreographer of Mortal Affairs for the Department of Anthropologism Commodore Rabelais will hear about this," he said indignantly. He began typing into the palmscreen of his vidglove. "This is going in my report."

Prague made a farting noise with his lips. "Put that in your report, too."

Administrator Wichita typed with added urgency. Maybe Prague had been wrong about his vidphone; with protracted neck, hardened potbelly, beaklike nose and sonorous voice, the Administrator rivaled Foghorn Leghorn rather well. He wasn't certain about the Administrator's affinity for troublemaking, though, a staple of the patriarchal, anthropomorphous rooster's day-to-day conduct. At any rate, Prague roundhoused his superior, softly, but hard enough to knock him cold, then flashed his badge and cut in line, signing the bare minimum of autographs without conveying a sense of excessive egomania...

In the long, fetid, gruesome tailwind of sky-fetishized terrorism, and in an effort to be environmentally chic and high-minded, kamikaze SAMSA pilots flew all of Amerika's airliners in a single file line across the Atlantic ocean and, one at a time, nosedived into select Scottish lochs, some of which measured up to four miles deep at their spines, until the airliners were officially extinct. Thereafter the Amerikan government "encouraged" the rest of the world to imitate the same destructive praxis at risk of "having the southern-fried Jesus nuked out of them" according to an out-of-the-corner-of-the-mouthism spoken by Amerikan President Grimley Bogue to his No. 2 bodyguard that was picked up by a puff of nanoscopic tabloid dust.

As an alternative to traditional, jet-propelled methods of long distance flight, the science fictionalized world turned to late French author Jules Verne, a forefather of the genre-cum-reality, although widely regarded as less imaginative and dynamic than contemporary and fellow forefather H. G. Wells, a prolific British didact whose scientific romances often violated the guile of cause and effekt. It was determined that Verne's ideas would be easier to bring to fruition. In his novel *De la terre à la lune* (trans. *From the Earth to the Moon*), Verne posited a gigantic columbiad, viz., a muzzle-loading cannon souped up in such a way that it could fire his protagonists onto the lunar surface. Pre-MAP decision-makers had reservations about the feasibility of the device, at least in terms of space travel; penetrating the earth's atmosphere required more propulsion than the average joehead realized. But there was no reason why it couldn't be manufactured and employed for strict terrestrial purposes, especially in the wake of the Great Loch Death Dive, not to mention the death of reality. Moreover, why use a cannon? Cannons required gunpowder. Cannons had to be smelted, rust-proofed, ignited and sponge-cleaned. Slingshots, on the other hand, could be composed of entirely non-volatile, eco-friendly materials. No deafening bang sound either. Strapped into the appropriate lounge chair, one would hardly notice the catapultic transition from ground to air...

"Ticket, please," droned the flight attendant as a new tranzbubble ballooned from a fissure in the slingpad. At full capacity the exterior of the tranzbubble solidified while a viscous lounge chair and a montage of gel-screens formed on the interior.

"Ticket, please," the flight attendant repeated. Prague scowled at his pillbox hat and said, "Tickets don't exist. Tickets haven't existed for thousands of years."

"Yessir." The flight attendant scanned his eyes. "Name: Vincent Prague. Codename: Vincent Prague. Title: Special Agent Anvil-in-Chief. Race: Noir Amerikan. Gender: Meta Male. Height: 6 Feet 8 Inches. Date of Birth: Unspecified. Eye Color: Transparent. Destination City: Prague, Former Czech Republik. Destination Slingpad: Prague Orange-45x. Tranzbubble Flavor: Extra Spicy Chicken Wings with Extra Blue Cheese and No Celery. Tranzbubble Blood Type: 18-Year-Old Single Malt Isle of Skye." Registering the flavor and blood type, the tranzbubble modified itself accordingly. "Did you know your name plagiarizes your destination? May I ask why you're going to Prague? What's in Prague that you can't find here?"

A bellowing arrival flew overhead and crashed into a knot of razorsharp antennae. Flourish of strings and percussion...The Anvil-in-Chief smiled. "I'm on a quest narrative, but I anticipate deviating from traditional quest patterns. I've already experienced several curious deviations. In any case, I'm the anti-hero. Protagonist and antagonist. Man and doppelgänger. One and the same."

The flight attendant made a sour face. "No reason to get smart, Mr Prague. Or literal, for that matter. I was only making small talk. Have you flown with us before?"

"Just aim this fucker and throw me across the pond. Don't forget my briefcase. Do the right thing, Mookie. Kill me and I'm coming back to getcha." A door in the tranzbubble irised open, he climbed in, and the door irised closed. The flight attendant retrieved his briefcase and placed it against the skin of the tranzbubble, which assimilated it. Then he scurried behind the slingatron's main control panel. He punched a big button. He fiddled with joysticks. He manipulated a plume of holographic image-swathes, locking the tranzbubble into place. He confirmed and reconfirmed the destination coordinates. And he crossed his fingers for luck.

Smell of vulcanized rubber. Sound of an elastic grunt, of a clanking trebuchet...

...of the wind in the willows...

...In the air, Prague watched six movies simultaneously on amoebic gel-screens while eating the inner walls of the tranzbubble and drinking its blood from an aortic valve. Like all movies, they fell headlong into the scikungfi genre, deploying other genres in small amounts either for artistic effekts or to (unsuccessfully) convey a sense of narrative depth. One movie in particular caught his eye, a remake of a stage adaptation of a commercial in which an *artiste* wearing an aluminum Vincent Prague mask loomed over a box of sentient detergent that emptied itself into a washing machine and set the timer. "You don't need Vincent Prague to wash your clothes," said the voice-over. "Speckled Enzymes will do it for you." Featured on the box cover was the image of another *artiste* in a Prague mask. He leaned against a ninety-sixth generation Camaro with an ostentatious whale fin. It was this whale fin that became a focal character in the subsequent stage adaptation of the commercial. Directed by the late method playwright Lofton Gitt in the early "Shiny Demon" period of his career, the play's title underwent a torturous evolution as a result of Gitt's chronic indecisiveness, but also because whenever producers decided they liked a title, he considered it a Tier One order of business to fuck with their sense of complacency. *Whale Fin Goes Hogwild!!!* was the final title authorized by Gitt during his lifetime, although it was posthumously revised on numerous occasions (*Whale Fin Goes Extremely Hogwild!!!*, *Whale Fin Fucking Kills the Whole Goddamned World!!!*, *Whale Fin vs. Special Agent Prague, Vrooom!!!*, *The Queequeg Factor*, *W Is for Whale Fin*, etc.) by the playwright's many offspring and heirs. The script of the stageplay remained fixed, however, until its appropriation by the machinery of Hollywood cinema. Pop filmmaker Buddy Napoleon went in a different direction, shifting the focus away from the antagonism of the Camaro's whale fin to that of an impish vigilante (a.k.a. The Undeniable Essence) hired to kill Vincent Prague by the Ministry of Applied Pressure. Napoleon reduced the whale fin's role to a thirty second symbolic encounter with a "Walrus Man" who attempted to sexually abuse the automotive accessory but was apprehended by the BILWM (Bureau of Investigators against Lascivious "Walrus Men") before any serious damage could be done. But the scene that the Anvil-in-Chief now watched had nothing to do with whale fins, "Walrus Men," the BILWM, a vigilante, or even Prague himself. It was a conversation between an alien with an exobrain in a bubble helmet and a Julie Andrews simulacrum whose apparel and personality fluctuated between Mary Poppins, Maria Von Trapp, and Victoria Grant.

"I come in peace," synthesized the alien.

"Like in that Dolph Lundgren film?" asked Maria Von Trapp. "Who names a film *I Come in Peace*? That's an assertion, not a title."

"What is Dolph Lundgren?"

"Only, like, the biggest badass that ever lived," said Mary Poppins.

"He's hot as balls, too," added Victoria Grant.

The alien removed its bubble and began to cough. For a moment it appeared as if it would suffocate, but it acclimatized. "What species of balls heat up to the degree that they are worthy of being deployed in the aforementioned simile?"

"What simile?" asked Maria Von Trapp.

"The one you used in that sentence. That one."

"Dolph Lundgren is a simile?" wondered Victoria Grant.

"Of a sort, I suppose," said Mary Poppins. "*The Amerikan Heretic Dictionary of Exegesized Poltergeists* explains that a simile is 'an instance of one thing representing (i.e. *standing for*) another thing, as in the context of a literary work.' That's the first definition, mind you. Whatever the case, we must think about this issue in terms of representation, i.e., what is it that Mr Lundgren *stands for*? Swedish pride? Cold War dick-swinging? Aryan wish-fulfillment? Mankind in general? All this is assuming Mr Lundgren is preceded by a *like* or *as*. Otherwise the man is sheer metaphor."

Electricity skimmed across the cerebral cortex of the alien's exobrain. "According to our records, Dolph Lundgren has been dead for over 8,000 years."

"Are you calling me a liar?" asked Maria Von Trapp.

"Is that question intended for me or one of your other personalities?" replied the alien.

"Spit spot."

A troupe of burlesques poured onto the gel-screen and everybody danced the Time Warp. Then the Julie Andrews simulacrum attacked the alien with a Xingyiquan crotch shot. It chased the move with an earsplitting Kwisatz Haderach weirding word. The alien's head exploded like a corn stalk, tendrils of gore spraying from its neck...

Prague sighed. The Julie Andrews didn't work for him—a poorly written character, he thought, and miscast to the hilt. Regarding the movie as a whole, it wasn't the first shitty cinematic depiction of his life, and it wouldn't be the last: at least 100 shitty Vincent Prague-inspired movies had been made in the last five years alone.

He waved a hand and the wall assimilated the gel-screens. He drank the tranzbubble's alcoholic blood in silence until it knocked him out.

He awoke to the sound of the flight attendant's voice: "Mr Prague. Wake up, Mr Prague. I might have tossed you a little to the left. Please don't be angry. Please don't come back from the dead and hurt me..."

# 11
## Araby (Re)viz[it]ed

The anguish and anger that marked its gaze fluctuated with its vision.

—I'll fix it, said the monster's companion. I promise.

—My prototypes weren't blind, replied the monster. There are no lilies on my brow. *Scheiße!*

—You're not blind. You're just not working properly. But you're new. Give yourself time to adjust.

A man with no arms and legs crawled out of a hole in the wall. He said:

—Welcome to Araby. My name's Rardion! But most citizens call me Mike.

The greeter came closer, moving across the floor on his stomach like an inchworm. He wore a striped onesie.

—Can I be of service? May I assist you in some peculiar way?

The monster flinched and said:

—*Pee*-culiar.

—Don't be afraid, said the monster's companion, squeezing its elbow. This is normal. When you enter a bazaar, you must expect to be accosted. You must expect to be accosted when you enter anything, anywhere. Granted, the greeter lacks extremities. But that's not unheard of. People have lacked extremities for eons.

The monster's companion removed his sungoggles.

—Ah! chirped the greeter. He rolled onto his back. Dr Teufelsdröchk! I didn't recognize you!

—It's bright out.

—*Willkommen zurück!* We've just received a fresh batch of artichokes, I'm told. Straight from Algiers!

—Extraordinary. This is my monster. It is a psychocoporeal fusion of John Keats and Adolph Hitler. I call it The Sans Merci. It's a working title. But I suspect the title may stick.

The greeter rolled his head and frowned at The Sans Merci.

—Pardon us.

The doktor sidestepped the greeter, shepherded the monster through a security gate...and experienced an epiphany.

—I know the function of bald people, he said. They signify what planets look like from afar. Thus they symbolize the distance between A and B. Hence they are unceasing reminders of cosmic vastness and the certainty of Blank Space.

Illogical epiphanies were chronic phenomena in Araby, the owners of which had rigged the bazaar with ceiling fans that continually sprinkled Total Rekall dust onto shoppers, prompting them to either remember fond but forgotten experiences or, more commonly, extract meaning from nothingness. The owners sought to manufacture an illusory sense of intelligence and imagination in shoppers. This, in turn, would lead to a heightened sense of selfhood. And a heightened sense of selfhood would generate a greater desire to consume Araby's various wares. It worked, for the most part, although sometimes shoppers devolved into mere *artiste*-like creatures, fleeing the bazaar in order to construct their own unrealized self-portraits on the canvas of life. But once a shopper left the premises, s/he ceased to fetishize *Künstlerroman* narratives and exhibit Joycean conduct.

The Total Rekall dust had no effekt on The Sans Merci.

—Artichokes, mumbled Dr Teufelsdröchk. Why would that stump think I wanted artichokes? Artichokes are for plebes and antisophisticants. Artichokes are the scum of the vegetable world. Artichokes are assholes that have been yanked inside-out.

—You said artichoke five times in a row.

—People repeat things. People let you down, too. Nothing more.

They sat on a T-Bar that lifted and ferried them across the skyscape of Araby to its neurorganic produce section. Dr Teufelsdröchk expounded on the benefits of neurorganic produce along the way. How it filled the gap between body and psyche. How it filtered the stream of consciousness. How it massaged the soft interstices of the brain...The Sans Merci ignored him. It stroked its mustache and stared at the commerce below. Hawkers in colorful cloaks whispered back and forth, up and down the aisles. Thin, brown, empty-handed women disappeared into red curtains and reappeared carrying buckets of wet celluloid. Piles of merchandise everywhere. And looming grandfather clocks. And long wooden platforms. And crackling torches. And, for added effekt, hundreds of drunken James Joyce androids whose mustaches, the monster surmised, were identical to its own...

—I hate this place, said Dr Teufelsdröchk. Joyce was nothing but a spud-eater. But they have the best fruits and vegetables in Prague. In the entire European landfill, I'd argue.

A shopper three T-Bars ahead slipped and fell. Two strongmen caught him in a bed sheet and cheerfully threw him in the air, twice, before letting him go.

The Sans Merci said:

—My buttocks ail me. Where are the gondolas?

—They fetishize Lo-Tech here. As everywhere. It's the nature of the postreal world.

—Why?

—Less glitz. More gusto.

The T-Bar descended to the floor and they got off. Dr Teufelsdröchk smoothed the wrinkles from his corduroy slacks and had another epiphany.

—I remember when I was in the fourth grade, he said dreamily. The haters fed me goulash. I gagged and smelled the breath of God. It was at this moment that I realized, for the first time, that I was *not* God.

He twitched.

—This way.

As they wandered down the aisles, The Sans Merci had to fight the urge to goosestep. It wasn't easy. His boots seemed to be alive, angry. Possessed. They leapt out in front of him like cats whose tails had been stepped on.

Dr Teufelsdröchk commended the monster's efforts and lectured it:

—One can think and look like a Nazi, but one must not act like a Nazi. Not in public life. This is a Brave New World, remember. Better to traipse from here to there like a lovelorn poet, as if the floor beneath your feet is a bed of roses and you are a virgin chasing after the summer breeze. Consider the opening words of Keats' "To Autumn": "Seasons of mist and mellow fruitfulness!" Convert that sentence into your gait. Become one with Keats—but keep the Führer close at hand...

The monster began to skip, clumsily at first, as if kneeless, then with a certain *legerdemain*. Then it tripped over its feet and collapsed.

Nearby a James Joyce had been sniffing keelings. It hurried over and assisted the monster to its feet with a cane. Clad in beret, cravat and rubber fishing trousers, the Joyce said:

—Are you all right? I like your uniform. Is that rayon? I like your shiny pegs, too. I have medals. I was a boy scout once. I almost made it to eagle scout. But I flew too close to the ceiling lights...Can I help you find something, sir?

—I'm blind, croaked the monster, groping...

The Joyce cocked its head. Blind? It removed a flask from its jacket and took a swig.

—Blind, like, literally? Or metaphorically? Or both? It hiccupped. Oedipus manifested dual states of blindness. King Lear as well. Actually that's not true. In each case, one state led to the other. Only after the patriarchs had gouged out their eyes could they adequately perceive history, social relations, the price of eggs, and so on. I can see that your eyes are in your head. Perhaps they don't work? Perhaps things are precisely as they appear.

The Joyce offered the monster a sip from the flask. It declined.

—You look familiar, the Joyce continued. Have we met? Have you ever seen the film *Time Cop*? Despite that mustache, you're the spitting image of JCVD. Jean-Claude Van Damme, I mean.

—Thank you, interjected Dr Teufelsdröchk. Thank you, no. We don't need any help. Thank you. Good day, etc.

He led the monster away.

—No need to thank me, sir. I didn't do anything.

The Joyce pocketed the flask and began to roll a cigarette.

The doktor paused.

—You know, you don't sound anything like James Joyce. He looked over his shoulder. Joyce was Irish. You have an Amerikan accent.

The Joyce made a frog face.

—Doesn't everybody have an Amerikan accent?

Dr Teufelsdröchk's eyes slurped back into his head. Epiphany:

—There are plants in the world. They grow out of the sand. Their hands reach for the sky. Beyond the sky, there is blackness. Beyond blackness, there is nothingness. Beyond nothingness, there is the Television Screen of Eternity. That is what becomes of us when we die. To the Screen we shall return.

—I understand, said The Sans Merci...and tackled the Joyce. They slid across the aisle and crashed into a stack of cantaloupes. The Joyce howled. The Sans Merci picked up a cantaloupe and slammed it into the android's head once...twice...three four five times...The cantaloupe was ripe and didn't break until the eleventh blow, but by then the Joyce's head had been reduced to pulp. A puddle of bright green blood expanded across the floor...

"Somebody put food coloring in that android's blood. Is that legal?" Dr Teufelsdröchk's first instinct was to stop the monster. But he came to his senses.

The lighting in the aisle turned green and an electromagnasal alarm went off. A team of managers blustered one at a time out of a tall, thin doorway, followed the scent of the alarm across Araby, and confronted the insurgents. The managers looked alike: short, bald, round-shouldered and potbellied in cheap button-down shirts with Barrymore collars and tight brown polyester breeches with white socks. Their noses were iron cones. Their eyes were pulsing lenticular slashes.

They surrounded The Sans Merci and Dr Teufelsdröchk in an orderly semicircle.

—We are the managers, said the managers.

—You will pay for that Joyce, said one manager.

—You will pay for that cantaloupe, said another manager.

—You will pay for the expense of a cleaning lady, said another manager.

—You will pay for the expense of managerial time squandered on invective, said another manager.

—The Law is the Law, said another manager. The rest of the managers nodded and said, None escape.

Dr Teufelsdröchk had an epiphany.

—We are the managers, repeated the managers.

—Words build bridges into unexplored regions, said The Sans Merci. And I do not see why man should not be just as cruel as nature. But I see nonetheless.

—Extraction!

Eyes flashing, the semicircle of managers lumbered forward, zombified, groaning, to collectively secure payment. The Sans Merci, of course, didn't own a bank account, let alone a dollar to its name. But the doktor's entire savings account could be accessed via his retinas, which, like all human retinas, had been registered with and wired to the WBAS (World Bank of the Amerikanized Soul) at birth. Who could tell how much the managers would take? Dr Teufelsdröchk cowered behind The Sans Merci.

...interrupted by a man with a goat head. Standing over seven feet tall, he wore sunglasses and a trench coat. He unbuttoned and opened the trench coat, exposing a liver-spotted torso infested with long, pink nipples and udders. The managers stiffened at the sight of the torso. And when the man said, Feeding time, they assailed him with vampiric fervor and desperation.

He tipped over onto his back and moaned as the managers sucked him dry... When they had finished, the man with the goat head stood, buttoned his trench coat, adjusted his sunglasses, snorted, combed his goatee, bowed, and walked away.

—And no birds sing, whispered The Sans Merci.

—Po-Tweet? said a manager, wiping secretions from his lips and chin. His colleagues screeched like pterodactyls.

They moved in...

Dr Teufelsdröchk told The Sans Merci to stop them.

—One at a time or all together?

—Either way. No matter what happens, I'm leaving this henhouse with a fistful of leeks. Remind me if I forget.

Nodding, The Sans Merci waited for the managers to get closer...and regurgitated on one of them. The manager shrieked as he dissolved, timelapsing into a pile of molten ash. It regurgitated on another manager; instead of melting, he caught fire and choked to death. A third manager exploded into a whimpering tornado of dust when the vomit touched him. Unnerved, yet undeterred, the remaining managers sallied forth...The Sans Merci tapped a Morse code onto the fingers of its left hand with a thumb. The humming red laserblades of a swastika burst from its knuckles. It dissected the managers at the waist in one swipe. Shiny brass tacks spilled from their open groins. A set of legs lurched towards a bed of sweet potatoes...

Dr Teufelsdröchk's palmphone rang. He looked at the miniscreen. Truth. He touched the miniscreen.

—Speak.

—Herr Doktor, said Truth. I've been looking all over for you. Where are you?

—Wherever I want to be.

—There's a problem. Beauty's hoarding grapes. How am I supposed to make the chicken salad?

—Why is it that you always call me? Why doesn't Beauty ever call me?

—He doesn't like to talk on the phone.

—Wizard of Wor! yelled a James Joyce, pointing at The Sans Merci. Several other Joyces crept onto the scene. So did a number of shoppers, vendors, and people in animal suits. Another electromagnasal alarm went off, summoning another team of managers. This time they brought pulsar swords...

—Spill your guts, Truth, said the doktor. Things are about to get prickly.

—Are you at the grocery store?

—Like I said, I'm wherever I want to be.

—Why are you at the grocery store? That's our job. Are you dissatisfied with your assistants' ability to procure victuals? Have we done something to offend you?

Following a series of hollow taunts, a manager lunged at The Sans Merci with a flaming pulsar sword. The android stepped aside. Too heavy for the manager to navigate, the sword swung around and fell on his shoulder, cutting halfway down his torso. Smell of fried cheese. A train of intestines chased the brass tacks out of his body.

...the green gore of a James Joyce sprayed Dr Teufelsdröchk. He wiped his eyes and palm clean and backtracked down the aisle.

—You two *Muschelesser* couldn't read a grocery list to save your lives! he shouted. You can't use the toilet without coming to blows. And you are *not* to be trusted. In fact, when I get home, I will rewrite your contract under the name Untruth. And Beauty will be revised to boot. You will be what you are, not what I want you to be. Untruth and Ugly.

Behind him, a rumbling, a bellowing, an erupting...

—I really think you're overreacting, Herr Doktor, said Untruth. Whatever happens, though, I assume we will continue to operate at the same pay grade?

—The architecture of the human soul defies comprehension, the doktor epiphanized. And yet one can only conceive of this defiance through the medium of comprehension. I use the term *medium* here interchangeably with the term *metaphor*. In other words, I am the fireplace within the domicile of the human soul. My logs burn. My flames hiss. My flesh is a memory made of glass.

—Be careful not to break it. Your mind will spill onto the earth.

Dr Teufelsdröchk made a fist and hung up on Untruth. Bending over, he scrutinized an urn of onions, selected one, stood and turned around...Gazing up into the darkness, he saw a creature driven by blindness and insight. He took a bite from the onion and his eyes began to burn.

# 12
## Statue of Libashout[2]

Prague noticed it on his descent as the tranzbubble started to disintegrate: a giant bronze statue of Franz Kafka in a bowler hat, dickey and sweater vest standing in the Vltava River. Over its head the statue brandished a great chainsword that hummed like a thousand helicopters and made woodchips out of passengers whose flight attendants had flung them off course...

---

2    "A simple existential observation that life is full of imperfections" (*Urban Dictionary*).

# 13
## Two Mad Assistants & Two Assistant Monsters

"We are only that which we are perceived to be," said Untruth. "At any rate, I would just as soon manifest the entire spectrum of my selfhood before I abide exclusively as one polar extreme. Truth and Untruth in chorus— that's me."

Beauty/Ugly raised the doppelgänger of his manicured eyebrow...

Dr Teufelsdröchk's laboratory smelled like burnt wigs and rotten catfish. Truth/Untruth flipped a switch. A loud stentorian voice said, "Perhaps we can frighten away the ghost of so many years ago with a little illumination. Gentlemen!" The pipes of an unseen organ commenced Andrew Lloyd Weber's *Phantom* and the laboratory came to life like a carnival at dusk...

Beneath the blue glow of an ichthyosaurus aquarium, it took them thirty minutes apiece to create surrogate monsters with their employer's monster-making kit. Both accomplished the task on the first try. The monsters resembled their makers except for minor phrenological and skeletal variations (e.g. they had scoliosis and walked at funny angles). Truth/Untruth and Beauty/Ugly dressed them in conventional, Nazi-chic *Sturmabteilung* attire: über-starched light brown shirt, flared dark brown jockey pants, and shiny knee-high moonboots with visor caps, collar and sleeve emblems, party pins, merit badges, and other *Deutschland Erwache* regalia.

"*Achtung!*" said Truth/Untruth.

The monsters looked at each other, then at Beauty/Ugly. Beauty/Ugly shrugged.

A sea cow swam into view and a school of ichthyosauri attacked it.

...soft nebula of blood and bowels...

# 14
## The Hotel Prague

He didn't miss the pillow, but he hit it awkwardly, briefcase-first. He rolled off, dodging at least six more new arrivals...

Slingpad Prague Orange-45x was downright somber compared to Slingpad Amerika 7-2521. No music here. No spotlights or fanfare or stiltwalkers. And almost nobody spoke. Veritable silence but for the *pft* and "Oof!" of bodies hitting pillows and the *zzzht* and "Aah!" of tranzbubbles being flung into the sky.

Surrounding the slingpad, a panoramic view of the city...Steel grays and pungent browns distinguished what looked like a giant, pried open set of shark's jaws. Flames hissed out of countless smokestacks. Thick bolts of electricity danced between the prongs and spikes of antennae. Buried beneath the neoindustrial spectacle, the pulse of oceanic discotheques, circuses, casinos, bazaars...

Prague walked to the edge of the slingpad and stepped off. He parachuted to the street.

He hailed a Mach GoGoGo. "To the Hotel Prague on Prague Street," he told the cartoon behind the wheel. The cartoon said, "Ja," adjusted its white helmet, tightened its red scarf and squealed into traffic. The faster it drove, the louder the *Speed Racer* theme song played on the vehicle's stereo.

Prague paid the cartoon with a deck of autographed 2x4s, got out of the GoGoGo and entered the hotel. A bellhop wearing a T-shirt with the image of Prague in a boy scout uniform on it greeted him. Beneath the image were four words: **Your Name Is Prague**.

The bellhop glanced down at the T-shirt, then at the Anvil-in-Chief. "My name's Prague, too. Henrí Prague." He reached for the briefcase. "May I?"

Prague waved him away. "Where'd you get that shirt? That shit isn't funny."

The bellhop blinked. "Funny? I don't understand. Humor has been outlawed in the Former Czech Republik. At any rate the shirt was a gift from Commodore Rabelais."

Frowning, the Anvil-in-Chief looked the bellhop up and down. The bellhop said, "I've already taken the liberty of checking you in under the name Codename Vincent Prague a.k.a. Vincent 'Codename' Prague. Per Commodore Rabelais' request, of course. We have booked you in the Galactic Pot-Healer Suite. Here is your key. Follow me, sir." They weaved through the golden slot machines and green blackjack tables of the lobby to an elevator that shot them to the 800th floor like a pinball. They emerged into an expansive room full of *Leave It to Beaver* and *Last of the Mohicans* and Canned Ham slot machines that turned users into brain-eating zombies after just a few hours of play. Henrí Prague gored and killed at least eight users with an ionized cattle prod as he led Vincent Prague across the room to a long hallway. At the end of the hallway loomed the tall mahogany doors of the Galactic Pot-Healer Suite.

Prague hesitated.

"Anything wrong, sir?" said the bellhop.

"I don't trust doors that don't iris open. Let alone doors made of wood."

"It is my understanding that you are a lover and aficionado of All Things Vintage."

"That's beside the point. Totally."

"The elevator doors didn't iris open. You didn't seem disturbed by them."

"An elevator is a box in motion. A hotel room is a box in limbo. Two different animals altogether."

The bellhop nodded.

Shaking his head, Prague tapped an electronic eye and the doors clicked open.

Inside the Galactic Pot-Healer Suite were the usual suspects: lamps, chaises, a bed, paintings of albatrosses, a hookah, useless accent furniture, a bronze statue of a dancing Kafkaesque beetle, dubious shadows...Something about the room unnerved Prague. It looked...sordid. Used. And yet luxurious, as if the room's furnishers had attempted to represent a metaphorically unclean aesthetic with state-of-the-art tools and fixtures. But what, specifically, was unclean? Prague couldn't figure it out.

"Per my instructions," said Henrí Prague, "your closet has been fully loaded with fashion statements from several time periods and measures of quality control. We are an affirmative action institution here at the Hotel Prague and emphasize diversity at every turn. I know you understand." He led the Anvil-in-Chief into the closet and walked him in a circle. Prague knelt on the floor, opened his briefcase and inspected its contents. Spare body parts seemed to be in order. He closed the briefcase and slid it under a biomechanical Nosferatu robe. They returned to the main antechamber.

A woman stood in the orange light of a lamp. She looked like Henrí Prague and possessed the same distended torso. Unlike Henrí, however, she wore a corset, garter belt and stiletto boots. Her breasts threatened to leap at any moment from asphyxiating binds. Her colorful, writhing hair fell over one shoulder in a plait of coral snakes. Prague wondered if they were real.

"They're artificial," said the woman. Prague wrinkled his lips. Was she a telepath? Did telepaths exist in the real world or only in books and films? Sometimes he forgot.

She ran a fingernail across the bulging arc of her breasts. "I had them filled with low-sodium peanut butter. You like?"

"I like peanut butter," said Prague.

Henrí Prague cleared his throat. "May I introduce my sister, Mädchen 'The Prague' Prague."

Her hips swung like a pendulum as she walked towards Prague and extended her wrist. He observed the wrist. "Why the hell's everybody named Prague? What the hell's going on over here?"

"We are in Prague," said the bellhop, puzzled.

"So everybody in Prague's named Prague? I don't think so."

"Your name is Prague as well," said the bellhop's sister, raising the fingers of her outstretched wrist and studying her nails. "How do you account for this absurdity?" Her voice was deep, masculine.

"It's not absurd. It's my parents' surname."

"As it is our parents' surname," she replied. "And our grandparents' surname. And our great grandparents' surname. *Und so weiter*." Her brother nodded with raised eyebrows, then excused himself.

"What's a Prague?" said Prague.

Mädchen smirked. "A Prague?"

"Your codename is 'The Prague.' What is it?"

She ran her hands up her thighs and made a noise that fell somewhere between contemplation and orgasm. "A chess piece?" She smiled like a horse. Her front tooth had a circular nicotine stain on it.

"You're asking me? That'd be a *pawn*, toots. Not a Prague."

Her smile disappeared. "You are so very aggressive. But that is what you Amerikans do. I like. Enough talk Mr Anvil Man. Walk this way."

He followed her into the bathroom, watching her ass go back and forth. As Cdre Rabelais promised before his excursion to the Former Czech Republik, Mädchen "The Prague" Prague served him breakfast (continental) at a side table and ran him a bath. She even washed his back, feet, cock, balls and asshole. A sentient towel dried him, scampering across his body, into his groin and armpits, sponging up every last bead of moisture; it concluded by scrubbing his hair dry and then wrapping itself around his head like a turban.

Mädchen took him by the penis and led him to the bed. He stiffened in her grip. With the stilettos she was about his height. She was thin, but strong; in the right light Prague could see muscular striations in her limbs. She clutched his neck and yanked back on his hair, calling his Adam's apple to attention. She licked the Adam's apple. She licked his chin, his lips. "I only let strangers fuck me in the ass," she rasped. "My cunt belongs to the city."

...She kissed him with eyes wide open. Her eyes grew wider and wider as the kiss deepened and Mädchen extracted payment for services-about-to-be-rendered. Prague let it happen. Sexual activity was the one thing the MAP comped...She pushed him onto the bed. He did an accidental somersault, coming face to face with his genitals, then smacked into the headboard. Pain. Vertigo. Things went dark. He saw Mädchen's tits emerge from behind a curtain. He caught a glimpse of her snatch, shaved, with a tattoo arched over the garage that read: VAGINA...He noticed for the first time a dumbwaiter in the wall. The rope squeaked as the carriage lowered and lowered and came into view and the door of the carriage irised open and twenty liters of roaches spilled into the Galactic Pot-Healer Suite. The carriage irised closed on the corroded head of the Nowhere Man...Mädchen comforted Prague with catlike purrs, stroking his limbs, his temples, ensuring his penis remained tumescent with martini juice.

"There was a man who fell asleep," he said, and turned over to fall asleep. She kidney-punched him. Crying out, he rolled off the bed, hit the floor with a loud thump.

"Be quiet up there!" said the tenants in the room beneath them, whacking their ceiling with a broomstick. "Our children are trying to sleep!"

Prague stood and answered the complaint with a series of stomps that cracked the floorboards. Mädchen leapt off the bed and rammed him with her shoulder. His legs kicked up and over his head and he landed on his back and lost his wind. Mädchen dragged him to the bed and poured a bottle of turpentine on his face. Prague choked, coughed, sobered. But his vision failed him: the head on her body oscillated between "The Prague" and the Nowhere Man, the latter of which melted like wax every time it materialized.

"I killed you," said Prague.

"Killed who?" said "The Prague."

"The Nowhere Man."

"I know dah-ling. Everybody knows."

"Nobody can kill Nowhere. It's impossible."

"The world is an endless lagoon of impossibilities." She rolled onto her stomach and grabbed the cheeks of her ass. "Now get to work."

He tarried. She hit him with a log.

"Where'd you get that log? Where'd that log come from?"

She hit him again and he slumped onto his back and she climbed on top of him and wedged the log between his chin and clavicle and shoved her ass onto his cock. The lights dimmed by themselves...

# 15
## The Delova Prague

He looked in the mirror and flexed his abs. The rumblestrip 8-pack was fantastic, hyperreal—an anatomical marvel resulting from a healthy combination of hard work and harder technology. Still, the abs were ill-defined in places; he counted four bloated nooks and one area with medium-intensity ripples. Nobody else would have noticed the glitches unless they had been underscored and explained. But he noticed, and that's what counted.

"Open Sesame." A slit formed beneath the sharp, clean ridge of his pectoral muscles. Wincing, he eased his fingers into the slit, fished around, and removed the Ab-Crab® inside. He scrutinized the expiration date. Two days to sour milk. Good timing. He tied its cords into a knot and threw it away. From his briefcase he removed another Ab-Crab® bound in bright gold packaging. He tore open the packaging and the Ab-Crab® leapt out. It landed on the bathroom counter, tripped and fell into the sink. Its anterior tendril terminated in a set of Rocky Horror lips. The lips squeaked, "Help me! Help meeee!" as the Ab-Crab®'s sclerites clicked against the porcelain like spilled marbles.

He picked the creature up by one of its legs. "Relax." The Ab-Crab® thanked him and asked about the weather. Then it began to take deep, controlled, overdramatic breaths, as if practicing yoga.

He stuffed the Ab-Crab® into the slit...

The slit sealed over. He doubled over.

Punches and kicks projected from his stomach. Alien screams rolled up his throat. He gripped the edge of the counter and tried not to vomit. He vomited. He punched the mirror. Cracks emanated from his fist in a burst of slow lightning.

His knuckles drooled blue...

It took the Ab-Crab® three or so minutes to settle in. Longer than usual. But eventually its pincers found purchase and his flesh shrinkwrapped against its exoskeleton. He admired the finished product in the mirror's fragments.

"I shoulda had a V8," said Codename Prague...

Before accompanying Mädchen "The Prague" Prague to The Delova Prague discotheque, he wanted to squeeze in a quick workout. He did 1,000 pushups on his thumbs and 500 index finger pullups. Then he undressed, put on a suit of medieval armor standing in the closet, clanked down the hallway and took an elevator to the hotel swimming pool. On the way he reconnoitered his mission...What was it? Rabelais had told him to go to Pragensia St Cagney, the casino beneath The Delova Prague, and await further instructions. From who? What about? Would he have to fight, torture or kill anybody? Who? How? Where? No doubt the whole mission would turn into the usual assfuck. His instructions would be to go somewhere else to get more instructions, and those instructions would instruct him to get instructions elsewhere, and the instructions he got elsewhere would point him in another direction, and so on until he was 1,000 years old, at which point Rabelais would summon him back to Amerika, tell him the mission was either a practical joke or a test of his allegiance, and present him with another carton of voodoo cigarettes. Whatever. He could take anything the MAP could dish out. He had prevailed before; he would prevail again.

The pool was empty except for a few overweight Arabs in keffiyehs and bikini briefs eating cheese and drinking absinthe at a corner table. He stood at the edge of the pool. He stared into the neon green water. A pale-skinned Culkin wearing a giant Hawaiian bathing suit appeared next to him. It looked up at the Anvil-in-Chief as if trying to see somebody on the top of a building.

"Hey mister."

Prague flipped open his eye shield. He rotated and angled down his torso. "Yes?" he said.

"Where'd you get that suit?"

"Compliments of the house."

The Culkin tapped his leg. It echoed.

Frightened, the Culkin ran away.

"Good boy."

Prague dove in the pool and did fifty lethargic laps, toes dragging against the bottom. Afterwards he did two shots of absinthe with the Arabs, then went back to his room and swapped the armor for a tux.

Mädchen appeared at his side. Now she wore a black *Breakfast at Tiffany's* cocktail dress with elbow-length gloves. Her hair lay atop her head like a sleeping cat; the snakes were gone. She had sprayed herself with black-and-white aerosol and resembled a silent film cutout. She smoked a long hashish pipe.

Prague offered her his arm. She took it. "Where've you been?" he said.

She blew smoke in his face. "I have been here. I have been there. What do you care, Mr Anvil Man?"

"Good point."

In the elevator, a man dressed as a cardboard letter P stared at them. "I'm the letter P," he said. "Guess what I stand for?" He whispered something in Mädchen's ear. She maintained a straight face.

A street zeppelin took them to the Delova Prague.

Vincent Prague rested his cheekbone against the window. Night fell and the manholes swallowed the day's smog. The city pulsed with meaning and energy. The cogs and sprockets and levers and girders of Purpose Engines spun and whirred and wooshed and clanked up and down the streets...They drove through Little Amerika. Sidewalks teemed with mummies and werewolves and toxic avengers and Lobster Men and Scarlett O'Haras and Richard Nixons and Jay Gatsbys and other B-film creatures and the zeppelin had to weave through a pinball playfield of corndog and hamburger and ice cream cone stands. Lizard music on the radio—bebop jazz with a dash of pickled electronika... Then they drove through Little Hong Kong and the zeppelin had to weave through Godzillas trying to stomp on them and shoot fireballs at them and hurl fistfuls of kamikaze Bruce Lees at them. Prague fell asleep...When he awoke

Mädchen was unzipping his pants with a pliers. She froze...She fed the pliers to her cleavage.

"We're here," she said pointedly.

Prague got out of the vehicle, zipped up his pants and signed the windshield with a bar of soap.

Ignoring Mädchen, he strode towards the discotheque.

A line of glitterati circled the building twice over. A few of them noticed Prague, but nobody asked for his autograph. He went to the front of the line.

An anabolic bouncer with a square head and Asimovian sideburns poked him in the chest. "I don't think so, sonny," it said in an out-of-order drone.

"Behave yourself," said Prague. He moved past the bouncer. The bouncer grabbed him by the shoulder and hurled him into the street.

Prague somersaulted through the air like a ragdoll...He landed on his hands, cartwheeled onto his feet. Instantly he was back in the bouncer's face. The glitterati behind him stirred and began to polish their guns.

He adjusted his bowtie. "Daddy used to toss me around like that." He scratched his temple with a thumbnail. "I fed him to the fuckin' pigs."

The bouncer said, "I know who you are. Piss off, meathead."

Before Mädchen could stop him, Prague trimmed the bouncer like a T-bone steak with a divining machete, the blade of which was electromagnetically attracted to fat cells...

They rode the wave of glitterati into the Delova Prague.

"Where there is cause there is effekt," said Mädchen over the robosyncretic cacophony of the discotheque. Lasers and bullets whizzed everywhere. "This is not Amerika. This is only Amerikana. You do not kill strangers here unless you have a good reason or unless you make it look like an accident. The Former Czech Republik is no place for futuristic gunslingers, swashbucklers, or knife throwers. Scikungfi is encouraged in theory but frowned upon in actuality."

Prague fingered his cuff links.

A woman walked towards them from the dance floor. She could have been Mädchen's twin except for certain physiognomic vagaries that Prague couldn't quite discern. The vagaries bewildered him to such a degree that he decided she looked nothing at all like Mädchen. What was wrong with him? First the hotel room, now this broad. Was he losing the ability to perceive life's small details? It worried him. Life's small details were all that mattered...

She wore a long Charmeuse bridal gown with a steam-ironed Morticia Addams hairdo parted down the middle. Like Mädchen, she had stylized herself in black-and-white. She introduced herself as Sindie Switch, kissed Mädchen on the lips, and gave Prague a small wooden box. "Open it," she said in a deep, deep tenor.

"It's locked."

"It is an ersatz lock. Purely decorative."

He opened the box.

Inside was a small assortment of strings. Bits of strings. Some of them had frayed ends. Some of them didn't.

"Either they are outmoded, or they are too short. They are mostly too short. The waste products of other strings. Residua. *Nachgeburt.* I can't find a use for them. I can't even tie them into knots. And yet I can't bring myself to throw them away."

She snatched the box. Before Prague could respond, she nibbled her lip and said, "I have lava in my veins."

"Bullshit," said Prague.

She slit her wrist. Steaming orange lava flowed out, dripped onto the floor and burnt a hole in it. The wound cauterized and scabbed over. She picked the scab off. She gave the scab to Mädchen along with the box and the items vanished into Mädchen's cleavage.

Prague nodded. "Nice trick. Is recess over yet? Let's get this road on the show."

And they fell on him, and they kissed and scratched and bit him, and they were dancing, and somebody wrenched Prague's penis from the shell of his pants...Strobe lights. Clove cigarettes. Technologized desire and a cyclone of neon voyeurism...Pushing air from his lips, Prague thought about dress ties as the femme fatales had their way with him. Not the paltry, winged nub beneath his Adam's apple, but the real things. Why did they exist? More importantly, how did they come into existence? MAP literature claimed they evolved from the French cravat. Ludicrous. At some point, deep in the graveyard of history, a man hung a strip of fabric from his neck, walked out into the world and called himself a man among lesser men, inciting a massive, masculine fashion craze. Neckties became a staple of everyday patriarchal life. And they served no purpose. They hung down the sunken chest of humanity like dead serpents waiting for somebody to bury them...

# 16
## Pragensia St Cagney

They took an escalator to the casino. It was four miles long and moved at a rate of approximately 5 mph. Prague stole another nap on the way down. He slept standing up. When he awoke...

A door irised open. They walked inside.

He doubletaked the giant head of a smiling, round-faced professor with pince nez and a gold-tasseled graduation cap. It was ES Lowe—founder and poster boy of Yahtzee. Hanging from the ceiling like an obese piñata, the head stared down at the crowd with archetypal panoptic efficiency...

"Yahtzee is a game of skill," said a Zero Punctuation Expobot. In addition to various anti-utilitarian James Cagney androids, ZPEs had been strategically positioned throughout Pragensia St Cagney. "To play Yahtzee one throws the dice and accomplishes Three-of-a-Kind or Four-of-a-Kind or a Full House or a Small Straight or a Large Straight or Chance or Yahtzee that's Five-of-a-Kind one may acquire as many Yahtzees as one wants in thirteen rounds but one may only acquire one of the aforementioned combinations and one must keep one's hands to oneself at all times if you require further exposition feel free to exposition and additionally exposition exposition thank you," said the ZPE.

Prague walked across the gambling floor of Pragensia St Cagney, reluctantly, flanked by his black-and-white escorts. They had nearly broken his stronghold of patience. But he would endure them for a little longer, at least until he received directions from somebody, or he got the hint that the gig was another MAP-sanctioned scam at his expense.

In Pragensia St Cagney, there were no roulette wheels. There were no craps or blackjack or Texas Hold'em tables. There weren't even slot machines. Stone coffins ran the length and breadth of the casino. Hunched over the coffins were the dried but sharp-dressed husks of the Elderly and the Plutocratic. Amid the cooperative chatter of Expobots, the shaking, the sliding, the clicking and the clacking of thousands of die...

"Who's in the coffins?" asked Prague.

"The fathers of reality," said Mädchen.

Emaciated pastel strippers in shadow boxes lined the walls. Only the Cagneys paid attention to them. Everybody else fixated on their respective Games of Skill.

"This way," said Sindie, gesturing across the casino. He followed the gesture's line of flight...and saw nothing.

Prague sidestepped the girls and pulled aside a Cagney. "Pragensia St Cagney. Why'd they name this place after you?"

"Why'd they name you after this city?"

"You know who I am?"

"Everybody knows who you are, sir. This is the world."

"Do you have something to tell me?"

"Dunno. Stay in school?"

"No. I mean, do you have a message for me?"

"Every spoken word is a message, Mr Prague. Inevitably my answer is yes. However, I believe you are looking for something else, or rather, an addendum, viz., something embedded within the already resonant topography of my discourse—a message within a message, as it were."

"Shh!" said a player at the table next to them. He threw the die and turned up Four-of-a-Kind in sixes. But he had recorded Four-of-a-Kind in threes five turns ago. And he had used his Chance throw two turns ago. He passed the cup to the next player and put a Walther to his head.

"Get wise on your own time." The Cagney slapped the Walther out of his hand. It flew over three tables into the hands of another Cagney who confiscated it.

Prague lost his patience. He cupped his hands over his mouth and shouted, "The name is Prague! Codename Prague! Who's got words for me! Heads up, shitforbrains! Daddy needs a new pair a shoes!"

At the exclamation, all of the shadow boxes swung open and, like equines from the starting gate, the strippers leapt out and converged on him. There were 80 or so of them and Mädchen and Sindie joined in the blitzkrieg...

"You crazy bitches," Prague exclaimed. "What am I, a one-eyed jack factory?"

A long scikungfi fight lapsed into sexual catastrophe. Prague tried to be a good sport about it even though he had only packed two spare sets of genitals....

...DEFIBRILLATION...homeostatis interrupted by visceral anarchy...cross-section of kidneys filtering and secreting metabolites in fasttime...collective moan à la Ecstasy/Dread/Power...NOWHERE MATRIX dissolved into Moth Man evolved into *daikaiju*...flailing limbs and tentacles...more tentacles...stench of open holes...collage of hardcore still shots—Vincent Prague exposed in unforgettable contortions of defense and subjugation...devolutionary grunt, masculinized aural fetishism...sensory deprivation/overload...Burroughsian scat..."exposition exposition exposition"...one-liner..."Yahtzee!"...coffin tipped over and out spilled...

The strippers retreated to their shadow boxes. Prague didn't bother picking up the scraps of his tux—it was destroyed. Naked and used, he delivered a sharp crowdstare to the room's many antagonists.

"Nice abs," chirped a Cagney...

He punched out Mädchen and Sindie. The strippers blitzed him again and he punched them out, too...Unblinking, unsmiling, the gamblers rolled the Yahtzee die...

In the end, Vincent Prague made the bad decision to flout his orders from that point on. He had done what Cdre Rabelais told him to do. Nothing panned out. He wasn't waiting there forever. He had things to do. He had a life. Being the Anvil-in-Chief didn't mean he couldn't enjoy himself from time to time. (Actually being any echelon of MAP-employed citizen meant that your ass was "not your own, ever, under any circumstance, imaginable or unimaginable, possible or impossible," as stipulated by the MAP's *How to Be a Person*

*Manual*, which was slammed onto the desktop of every new hire on Day 1. Nevertheless—Prague would do as he pleased. Despite setbacks, he always did as he pleased. He was Vincent Prague, celebrity, superstar, esquire, equerry, chevalier, jonkheer, vicar, anti-Tirthankar, Ali Baba, architect of sociotechnicity, primate *extraordinaire*, etc....And while visiting his metropolitan namesake he would catch a show. At one point theater had been like second nature to him. He had attended at least 5,000 Andrew Lloyd Weber productions alone. *Jesus Christ Superstar*, *Phantom* and especially *Cats* were his favorites. He always cried when Grizabella sang "Memory." When had he last seen *Cats*? And why had it been so long ago? He suspected it had to do with exposition exposition exposition expo...)...

# 429

## AR

After reality, roaring helicopters peel the skin from the sky like a grapefruit and reveal the pulp of outer space. The helicopters appear indiscriminately, dumping WMDs and cat-eyed David Bowie simulacra in equal measures onto the pale earth...

After reality, there will be no exposition, i.e., no exorcism of the ghosts from the narrative of the Body Dildonic...Lincoln Hawk beats Bully Hurly? Life as a spectacle of one armwrestling match after another set to the music-in-the-heavens of Kenny Loggins? Only in reality. After reality, Mr Hurly will rise up and over the top like a chunk of foam in the Dead Sea. Life jackets, however, will only be distributed on a need-to-float basis...

Crazy sentence here with a big period at the end of it<<<.>>>

FACT: Anything can happen anytime. Anybody is capable of anything.

FICTION: Nobody can exist nowhere. Nothing assumes the existence of something.

FICTION (REVISED): <<<.>>>

ELEVATOR PITCH: Michael Jackson kills and cryogenically freezes himself, unable to bear further vilification from the Papanazi. In his will he donates the remains of the Elephant Man (a.k.a. Joseph Merrick) to the United Arab Emirates, the governing powers of which have always detected mystical powers in Merrick's calamitous deformity. Somehow they will harness those powers and become the world's next Global Hegemon. The remains are stolen en route, however, by a mad scientist with a figurative cleft palate who has contracted a PT Barnum fetish. [Briefly contextualize Ringling Bros. and Barnum & Bailey Circus]. Long scikungfi fight here. Then the scientist reanimates the hideous corpse and hangs it on a hook in his laboratory, Leatherface-style. It squirms there for three weeks. Enter love interest. At first she's hesitant but eventually she loosens up and goes down on him and [Mad Lib]. After two weeks she dies of IFIEM (Irrational Fear of Impaled Elephant Men). Three weeks later Merrick squirms loose, eats the scientist's brains, and staggers to the North Pole, searching for the King of Pop. Secret agent men chase him. Vague selections from the *Bad* album emanate from distant icebergs. The secret agent men fall into the water and drown. The zombified Merrick presses on and disappears in an arctic gust of *qanuk*.

Fin.

"*Hajime!*" screeches a sensei. Tori administers a spine-shattering *tiatoshi* to his uke, then stabs him with a kodachi sword. Geyser of Hammer blood...

...irregular world without regulation. Diegesis of negative capability and the clockwork of truth.

# 17
## The Sans Merci vs. Macavity the Master Criminal

A flickering, pale green stripe passed across the screen of existence...

"Cats don't have nine lives," said the Truth/Untruth monster. "It's imprudent to think they do. Strangle a cat, if you don't believe me. It'll die. Once."

The Beauty/Ugly monster made a sad face. "I like cats."

...lights blinked on and off, on and off. Theatergoers scarfed down ice cream treats and located their seats.

Idle conversation petered into jaded whispers petered into primordial silence. The slot machines cleared their aluminum throats and donned silencers. "Tk-tk-tk-tk-tk-tk," went the maestro's baton.

Darkness.

A squad of naked globetrotters dribbled overinflated neon cat's eyes across the proscenium stage.

Silence.

Mischievous instruments: flutes, cymbals, synthesizers—their song allegorizing a cornfield at night. Every ear of corn an alive, angry *cobb dentata*...

The moon. The stars. Powerful blasts of catnip...

ACT I: When Cats Are Maddened by the Midnight Dance...During the first number, "Jellicle Songs for Jellicle Cats," the players flooded the stage, strutting, prancing, shadow-clawing, hitting low and high notes with varying degrees of success. They looked the same as always, just as they did BAR (Before After Reality)—ballerinas and Cooper Nielsens in tights and overdone cat makeup—with the exception of a giant TS Eliot robot and scores of vibrating

Bolshevik scythes and giraffe cannons. Spawn armor encased the cats' flesh as they attacked the robot and reduced it to a heap of molten shit. The Eliot killed a few of the players during the battle, and the audience clicked fingers as the Deceased's stark red blood flowed across the stage into the orchestra pit, stifling the jovial blurts of tubas, saxophones and French horns.

Humans had been barred from stage acting long ago by FCR Law. The government never specified why. Nobody cared—except for a handful of out-of-work actors who found employment in the Theater of Postblanketyblank Life.

...The Naming of Cats. The Invitation to the Jellicle Ball. The Old Gumbie Cat. The Rum Tug Tugger.

The Ugly/Beauty monster whispered, "Rum Tug Tugger's hogging the dance floor. He's too much! He keeps sticking out his tongue. He's, like, Dr Frank-N-Fürter or something."

"Shh!" said the Truth/Untruth monster.

...Mungojerrie and Rumpleteazer. Old Deuteronomy. The Awful Battle of the Pekes and the Pollicles.

..."What's a Pollicle?"

"Shhhhhhhhhhh!"...

During intermission, the casino games and slots fired up and a janitorial crew hosed the gore off the stage. They had goat heads.

ACT II: Why Will the Summer Day Delay—When Will Time Flow Away?...The Moments of Happiness. Gus: The Theater Cat. Growltiger's Last Stand. Dr Moreau's Vivisectional Romp (Recently Added Song & Flimflam/Scikungfi Dance) in which Mr Mistoffelees' Machinic Assistant Removes his Facial Tissue with a Scalpel & Sprays Glistening Hairballs from a Gash in his Navel...

Macavity "The Master Criminal" Cat. It appeared only for a moment. It bore resemblance to an old glamrocker with teased mane, impossible eyeshadow, crotchrocket glitterslacks, Holy Diver chest hair, and throbbing erect tail. "*Achtung*, muthafuckaaaaaahs!" it bellowed, ejaculating from multiple orifices, and then disappeared in an explosion of dead rodents. A herd of pussycat-strippers sashayed onstage. They tore off fans and folds and fishnets of lingerie and performed a series of synchronized splits and contortions and sex acts while singing about the dastardliness of Macavity Cat.

Halfway through the number a stranger wandered onto the stage. Clearly not part of the show. No makeup, with ghostwhite skin in the carbuncular light of the theater. Medals that dinged like wind chimes hung from a black, skintight suit. A lean mustache punctuated the stranger's overlip.

Bouncers retaliated with exigency. They leapt at the stranger from offstage, descended on the stranger from the rafters, lunged at the stranger from trap doors. The stranger dealt with each bouncer in turn, breaking backs, legs, necks with hammer-fast punches and kicks.

Suddenly the stranger was center stage. The music stopped. The pussycat-strippers stopped.

Silence.

Somebody said, "Is that Jean-Claude Van Damme?"

"Where did Macavity go?" the stranger asked the audience in an affected accent. "I empathize deeply with this character."

"Psst," said a voice from the foot of the main aisle. "Get the hell off of there. *Sofort!*"

The stranger glanced down. "I'm not leaving this stage until I talk to Macavity Cat, Dr Teufelsdröchk."

Dr Teufelsdröchk peered over his shoulder and giggled nervously at the audience. He eyeballed The Sans Merci and motioned it offstage with an exaggerated jerk of his head.

The Sans Merci folded arms across chest. Another bouncer attacked it. The Sans Merci clean-pressed the bouncer over its head and ripped him in half. Tic Tacs tinkled across the stage.

Fingers clicked.

Dr Teufelsdröchk rolled a program into a cone, put it to his mouth and said, "I knew it was a bad idea to take you to the theater. This is what I get for trying to enculture a friend. Grief. Absurdist grief."

"Is this part of the show?" asked the Ugly/Beauty monster. The monster's companion rolled a program into a cone, put it to its mouth and said, "No."

Nobody spoke for a long time. The Sans Merci and Dr Teufelsdröchk stared defiantly at each other as the machinic cat people cleaned hands and feet with tongues and the spectators buried their noses in paperback novels with dynamic cover illustrations and large black dots on every page...Finally Macavity Cat slouched onstage gripping a bottle of Jim Beam by the neck. It had skinned Old Deuteronomy and draped the patriarch's blood-spattered pelt over its shoulders.

"Hello," said The Sans Merci. "I am The Sans Merci."

Macavity took a swig of bourbon and slurred, "What's a Sans Merci?"

Dramatic pause............"It is why I sojourn here," the monster replied, "alone and palely loitering, though the sedge is wither'd from the lake, and no birds sing."

"I don't know what that means," said Macavity. "Look. Beat it, weirdo. We're in the middle of a goddamn musical."

The Sans Merci sucked in its cheeks. "I thought we might talk a little. I am a fine conversationalist. I can talk about anything. Incidentally I can *do* anything. I can write poems, and I can commit genocide. And I can do everything in between. Which is in fact *everything*, is it not? Existence as the gulf that divides a poem from a holocaust—that is my philosophy, my ideology, my ontology."

"Are you retarded? Somebody get this retard off my stage!" Macavity gesticulated at the production manager. Helpless, the production manager gesticulated back at him from behind the curtain.

"He's not disabled," proclaimed Dr Teufelsdröchk. "He's home schooled. Don't be so hard on him. He's only been alive for a few days."

"My queen!" bellowed The Sans Merci.

"Queen my ass." Macavity smashed the whiskey bottle against the head of Skimbleshanks, who was standing next to it. A computerized meow escaped Skimbleshanks and the cat hit the stage like a bag of snooker balls. Macavity pointed the jagged bottleneck at The Sans Merci and made a clumsy cutting motion.

Dr Teufelsdröchk said, "Leave him alone! You're drunk!"

"Please desist, sir," whispered the maestro to the doktor from the orchestra pit. "Never aggravate an actor."

The audience turned the pages of their paperbacks from one black dot to another.

"Aggravate who? Macavity? He's not the one you should worry about aggravating."

"Your fly is open, sir."

Dr Teufelsdröchk blushed and zipped up his pants.

"I'm going to the lavatory," said the Ugly/Beauty monster, getting up from its seat. The Truth/Untruth monster stopped it.

"You're an android," it said. "Androids don't use the lavatory."

"I can use the lavatory if I want to. There are all kinds of things you can do in the lavatory."

"Who calls a lavatory a lavatory? It's the toilet. It's the loo. It's the water closet. It's the vay-say. It's the restroom. It's the shitter. It's the head…"

"…Please, Mr Macavity. I don't want to hurt you. I just want to be friends with you," said The Sans Merci.

"Hurt me? Do you know how many nicknames I have? The Mystery Cat. The Not There Cat. The Un-Cat Cat. The Hidden Paw. The Napoleon of Crime. Sherlock's Anus. The Sasquatch of Irk. Lord of the Chicken Dance. Diddly Do-Wrong. Eliot's Id. Prufrock's Suplex. Boo-Yah of the Waste Land. The Illusory Fairy Rebuke. The Screaming Raw Dog. Kiss of the Barbed Wire Fist. Bizarro Mike. Eurotrash Jack. Overbaked Vampire Penetration. Seventy-Thousand Grasshoppers' Unfathomable Collective Hangnail Fury. The Well-Moistened Crabgrass Stomper…Get the picture? Nobody hurts a cunt with that many nicknames. I hurt you, see? I am the Way the World Ends. Not with a bang, not with a whimper—but with a cliché. Translation: Blow it out your ass."

"No more swearing!" insisted the production director. "Especially the c-word. It's misogynist!"

"Representation as critique," epiphanized Codename Vincent Prague. The Anvil-in-Chief sat ten rows behind Dr Teufelsdröchk's assistants' monsters and remained one of the few spectators who had not surrogated boredom with a plotless, wordless novel. In his periphery, ushers did wind sprints up and down the aisles, timing themselves with stopwatches, passing off flashlights like batons…

The Sans Merci made every effort to befriend Macavity Cat, even as Macavity stabbed at the android with the bottleneck. The scene transcended ridiculousness. Then, parrying a blow, The Sans Merci accidentally struck Macavity Cat on the forearm with the blade of its hand in such a way that Macavity's elbow and wrist exploded and its radius and ulna shot out of the forearm in opposite directions like two possessed chopsticks. The radius skewered a stagehand. The ulna smashed a Tiffany lamp offstage.

Macavity's forearm dangled from the ramparts of its elbow like a dirty sock. It ogled the hideous wound. It ogled The Sans Merci. "You think this means something?" it spat. "You think you've won? I don't give a shit about this!"

"That's the problem," breathed The Sans Merci. "Apathy. An epidemic of apathy. And a deprivation of camaraderie."

Dr Teufelsdröchk said, "Don't fancify your discourse. Be more colloquial, i.e., instead of saying 'a deprivation of camaraderie,' say, 'nobody likes one another.' But it's simply not true. People like people. Some do. I like you, for instance. I'm your comrade. I care about things, too."

"You only care about two things: the perpetration of food, and your lack of acclaim for the perpetration of food. And you're not my comrade. You're my master. You're my maker."

"Master? Let's not use that word. Let's say I'm your benefactor, or your mentor. That sounds nicer, doesn't it?"

An usher dropped a flashlight and slipped on it. The *faux pas* started a chain reaction. The usher toppled onto a spectator. The spectator dropped his novel and bumped into the spectator next to him. That spectator dropped her novel and bumped into her neighbor, who dropped his novel. And so on. A wave of novel dropping spread across the theater. It triggered other modes of asynchronous dropping. Musicians dropping instruments. Blackjack dealers dropping chips. Makeup technicians dropping hairdryers. And so on. The communal gaffe was brought to a conclusion by a possum dropping from the ceiling onto the stage between The Sans Merci and Macavity Cat. The possum wasn't dead. It struggled for breath. The Sans Merci pitied it.

Shrugging off the pelt of Old Deuteronomy, Macavity Cat stomped on it. The possum deflated like a football.

...The Sans Merci skinned and defleshed Macavity Cat with makeshift Wermacht daggers that morphed from its fingernails.

The razorwire skeleton beneath Macavity's hide was more anthropoid than human or feline. Two broad, membranous wings sprouted from its thorax. Macavity took flight, did three revolutions around the heavens of the theater to gain momentum, then kamikazed into The Sans Merci...They rolled across the stage and out of view. There was a backstage brawl that the theatergoers, lacking the energy or desire to retrieve their reading material from the floor, listened to with a modicum of curiosity. They clicked when Macavity's skeleton was hurled back onto the stage in pieces. The Sans Merci reappeared. The overdecorated shirt of its uniform had been torn off, revealing an impressive hypermuscular torso that bled from deep scratches. A caricature of The Sans Merci's own face had been tattooed onto its chest.

One piece of Macavity Cat was still alive. The Sans Merci finished the player in a feat of extreme ekphrasis...

Until now, Codename Prague had more or less enjoyed the play-that-wasn't-a-play-within-the-play, even if it didn't make sense. Just being at the theater again felt good. But the manner in which The Sans Merci had executed Macavity Cat riled him. He stood and shouted, "You can't do that! That sort of ekphrasis isn't ————! I don't care what country this is! You're under arrest! I'm taking you to Amerika!"

"I've never been to Amerika!" said The Sans Merci.

"Leave him alone!" said Dr Teufelsdröchk.

"What's an ekphrasis!" said the Beauty/Ugly monster.

"It's a graphic, ultraviolent depiction of a visual work of reality!'" said an usher.

"That's Vincent Prague!" said a nobody.

"Can I have your autograph!" said a nobody.

"*Anshlag!*" said the production manager.

"Do they have poets in Amerika!" said The Sans Merci.

"Poetry died with the modernists!" said an usher.

"The poet laureates of the postreal era are rappers, country music singers, car salesmen and people who make their mouths into big O-shapes!" said a percussionist. "Like this!" He made his mouth into an O-shape.

"Get your ass down here!" said Codename Prague.

"The institution that is now erroneously called the State generally classifies people only into two groups: citizens and aliens!" said The Sans Merci.

"What's he talking about!" said a nobody.

"It's a mnemonic flashback!" said Dr Teufelsdröchk. "It's perfectly normal!"

"The projection of memory is a symptom of insanity!" said a stagehand.

"Ditto!" said Bustopher Jones.

"Get your hands in the air!" said Codename Prague.

"Saturn is fallen, am I too to fall?" said The Sans Merci.

"Don't make me come up there and get you!" said Codename Prague.

"*Kumite!*" said The Sans Merci.

"Ekphrasis!" said Codename Prague. He stormed down the aisle.

"Ruuun!" said Dr Teufelsdröchk.

Everybody took the doktor seriously; cats and band members and spectators and ushers and even the production manager and his entourage ran out of the theater in a crazed exodus. The Sans Merci darted offstage. Codename Prague chased after him. Dr Teufelsdröchk turned and threw up his arms and shook his head at the empty theater. Empty except for two monsters, one of which waved at him.

"Wha—?" Stunned, he marched up the aisle. "Who are you? You are not my assistants. You are imposters."

The Truth/Untruth monster frowned. "How can you tell the difference?"

"I know the difference," snapped the doktor. "Difference is the payload of identity..."

# 20
## In Outer Space, a Ceramic Mannequin without Arms & a Cracked Foot

tumbled into a Disnified black hole.

And Dr Hans Reinhart said, "Something caused all this. But what caused... the cause?"

# 29
## Passagenwerk

[EDITORIAL NOTE: This chapter should be deleted from the book. Or this chapter should be the whole book. Don't fuck with your readers, moron.][3]

"The nonexistent text is the subject of the present study." Susan Buck-Morss, *The Dialectics of Seeing* (1989).

"The figure of wax is properly the setting wherein the appearance <*Schein*> of humanity outdoes itself. In the wax figure, that is, the surface area, complexion, and coloration of the human being are all rendered with such perfect and unsurpassable exactitude that this reproduction of human appearance itself is outdone, and now the mannequin incarnates nothing but the hideous, cunning mediation between costume and viscera." Walter Benjamin, *Passagenwerk*, trans. *The Arcades Project* (1927-40). Ref. Dorian Huckster's *The Man Who Lacked Digits* (4,501 AR) in which the protagonist wears viscera on the exterior of his costume after replacing his internal organs with "dire plumes of indecision."

"Under the strange nebulous envelopment, wherein our [Doktor] has now shrouded himself, no doubt but his spiritual nature is nevertheless progressive, and growing: for how can the 'Son of Time,' in any case, stand still? We behold him, through those dim years, in a state of crisis, of transition: his mad Pilgrimings, and general [dis]solution into aimless Discontinuity, what is all

---

3    Sig. Stanley Ashenbach.

this but a mad Fermentation; wherefrom, the fiercer it is, the clearer product will one day evolve itself?" Thomas Carlyle, *Sartor Resartus* (1830-31).

"A poet is the most unpoetical of any thing in existence, because he has no identity, he is continually in for—and filling—some other body. The sun, the moon, the sea, and men and women who are creatures of impulse, are poetical, and have about them an unchangeable attribute; the poet has none, no identity...[image of a flaccid penis]...If, then, he has no self, and if I am a poet, where is the wonder that I should say I would write no more?...But even now I am perhaps not speaking from myself, but from some character in whose soul I now live. I am sure, however, that this next sentence is from myself. I feel your anxiety..." John Keats, Letter to Richard Woodhouse (1818).

To what degree does sexuality figure into the narratives of Dr Seuss? Note how virtually all of his characters resemble sex organs that have been hacked or ripped off of their host bodies. (Ref. Jean-Luis Sçrapenut for a discussion of genital mutilation rep. comic/cartoon humanoids.)

"Macavity, Macavity, there's no one like Macavity, / There never was a Cat of such deceitfulness and suavity. / He always has an alibi, and one or two to spare: / At whatever time the deed took place—MACAVITY WASN'T THERE! / And they say that all the Cats whose wicked deeds are widely known /... Are nothing more than agents for the Cat who all the time / Just controls their operations: the Napoleon of Crime!" TS Eliot, *Old Possum's Book of Practical Cats* (1939).

"iFFFFPFP."[4] Adolph Hitler, Obersalzberg (1942).

"Since Hitler's day the armory of technical devices at the disposal of the would-be dictator has been considerably enlarged. As well as the radio, the loudspeaker, the moving picture camera and the rotary press, the contemporary propagandist

---

4    According to Kevin Taylor's *KA-BOOM!: A Dictionary of Comic Book Words, Symbols & Onomatopoeia* (2007), "The sound of a tuba player sucking in air" (39).

can make use of television to broadcast the image as well as the voice of his client, and can record both image and voice on spools of magnetic tape. Thanks to technological progress, Big Brother can now be almost as omnipresent as God. Nor is it only on the technical front that the hand of the would-be dictator has been strengthened. Since Hitler's day a great deal of work has been carried out in those fields of applied psychology and neurology which are the special province of the propagandist, the indoctrinator and the brainwasher. In the past these specialists in the art of changing people's minds were empiricists. By a method of trial and error they had worked out a number of techniques and procedures, which they used very effe[k]tively without, however, knowing precisely why they were effe[k]-tive. Today the art of mind-control is in the process of becoming a science. The practitioners of this science know what they are doing and why. They are guided in their work by theories and hypotheses solidly established on a massive foundation of experimental evidence. Thanks to the new insights and the new techniques made possible by these insights, the nightmare that was 'all but realized by Hitler's totalitarian system' may soon be completely realizable." Aldous Huxley, *Brave New World Revisited* (1958).

The pop culture apocalypse inculcates endless unspoken certainties. But the real problems stem from the uncertainties that onanistic talking heads articulate without possessing a mature enough historical, epistemological or linguistic character. Singing like a caged bird is for evolved drag queens. One must speak before one can sing. A bleached white wiggerization of the human condition usurps all forms of erudition. Popsong dreams + juvenile scenarios/episodes/dialogue/ant(I)gyros + high modernist mxyzptlk. The only cure is Liquid Panic. Thus the cry of the Wichita Lineman: "I can [only] hear you through the [wine]..."

"But how many solar anuses does a clockwork man require to achieve the perfect fulguration? One likes to at least approach perfection in this regard. As Georges Bataille writes: 'Yakety yakety Français blah blah blah Français blankety blank Français Français *nom de plume* et *mise en abyme* et cock-a-doodle-do etc. etc.' This passage effe[k]tively illustrates the *Dieselmotor* of all written, imagistic and oral texts and the authors that produce them. More importantly, Bataille provides us with a schematic for a healthier form of suicide. One doesn't like to kill oneself in an unhygienic fashion. One likes clean hands, empty bowels, and so forth." Betty Lomax, Inventor of the Somethingorother Machine (1,490 AR).

"Upon my asking what the word *urinate* reminded her of, she replied: *terminate*, the eyes, with a razor, something red, the sun." Georges Bataille, trans. Joachim Neugroschel, *Story of the Eye* (1928).

"No more than three glasses of wine or three beers per week." Jørgen de Mey via ghost writer Scott Hays, *The Action Hero Body* (2005).

Apropos L. Ron Hubbard in *Dianetics* (1950): "the scent of turkey might not only smell good to everybody, it might smell good on the same olfactory wavelength to everybody, assuming that everybody has dianetically rinsed (and thus optimized) their minds of all fruitless aberrations (e.g. neuroses, phobias, psychoses, etc.) and become *clears*. The[5] problem[6] with[7] life[8] is[9] the[10]

---

5    Definite article placed before a noun designating that noun with a certain specificity.

6    Synonym for *difficulty* or *conundrum*.

7    Preposition denoting an act of accompaniment.

8    The temporal, spatial and psychic realm inhabited by organisms. Alternately a "thing" or a "game."

9    Verb—present tense of *was*.

10    See note 5.

noncleared[11] individual[12] or[13] *aberree.*[14]" Ref. Hubbard's incl. of footnoted "words that are sometimes misunderstood...as an aid to the reader....Other definitions can be found in various dictionaries" (ix).

Sound of a Revving Motorcycle. Sam Waterson, *Law & Order* (1994-2033). Recall Waterson as Nick Calloway in *The Great Gatsby* (1974) and his contention that "the role was demanding. I've never had to try on so many white suits in my life. And they all itched something terrible. That's why I refer to 1974 as the Year of the Itchy White Suits whenever 1974 pops up in conversation."

"Laughing with increasing animation, I turn on the faucet, dampen a washcloth in warm water and begin to remove the makeup. The mascara, the lipstick, this powdery white mask—I wipe it from the skin of my face. THE END." DH Anonymous, *I, Alex* (1996).

"THE WIDE WORLD NO. 1. Mixing with the thousand pursuits & passions & objects of the world as personified by Imagination is profitable & entertaining. These pages are intended at this their commencement to contain a record of new thoughts (when they occur); for a receptacle of all the old ideas that partial but peculiar peepings at antiquity can furnish or furbish; for tablet to save the wear & tear of weak Memory & in short for all the various purposes & utility real or imaginary which are usually comprehended under that comprehensive title *Common Place Book.*" Ralph Waldo Emerson, Journal (1820). Emerson had an asymmetrical face.

---

11    Made-up compound word denoting the opposite of *cleared.*

12    Jeff "The Dude" Lebowski.

13    Conjunction unlike *and* or *but* that connects two or more alteries in a similar context.

14    Improvised, clipped, personified, nominalized version of *aberration.*

"The question mark is what's interesting. The answer is stupid." Hampton Fancher, *Dangerous Days: Making Blade Runner* (2007).

"Within its alkaline walls I uncovered deserts of vast paternities. They stood in a circle and fucked one another. I was taken aback. I wasn't expecting this. Outside the scream of a hog unseated the smalltalk of birds. I remembered the Netherlands. I remembered the afterlife. Furniture is an adequate means of reposition—that's what I told myself. I wanted to know why they were so hotly engaged in sexual congress. I placed a megaphone to my lips and asked them. My question unseated the scream of the hog. Then I felt the kiss of a tire iron on my exposed, pulsing, purple cerebellum." Danny Ikea, *The Psychic Ramparts of Trailer Fantasies* (1,700,025 AR)

"It's dark." Figure from the Dark Ages (c. 475-1000)

"I just shake the buildings out of my sleeves." Frank Lloyd Wright, Source and Date Unknown.

"Everything went to [expletive] when the Greenbergs came home and caught me taking a nap in their bed. <*Laughs.*> My freezer door was halfway open. I tried to close it, but gravity wouldn't let me, and a pack of fudgesicles was in the way. Anyhow the gig was up. <*Sighs.*> They beat me with sledgehammers, ate my internal organs, and threw me in a dumpster. After that it was life on the streets. <*Swears.*> <*Swears again.*> I hope those [expletive] eat [expletive] and [expletive] and burn in bleeping hell. <*Swears again.*>" Sentient Refrigerator, *My Life as a Sentient Refrigerator* (2207).

The production of writing is the production of a code. That goes for any production. To produce something is to encode it. Everything else entails an act of decoding, denuding, *deleuzing...*

"And a rinky dinky do to you!" Hong Kong Phooey voice-over perf. Scatman Crothers, *Hong Kong Phooey* (1974-76). Crothers passed away in 1986 at the age of 76. His name has nothing to do with feces or scatology but is a ref. to scat singing. Jack Nicholson nailed him in the chest with an ax in *The Shining* (1980). Hammer blood surged from the wound. Crothers played the drums in a speakeasy. He appeared on *Sanford & Son* (1972-77) and did a ski-dat-ba-bi-ba-dop-pop-pop with Redd Foxx. He appeared in *Zapped!* (1982), starring Scott Baio, and *Coonskin* (1975), starring an animated African-American rabbit. He reified yet problematized African-Amerikan stereotypes. He didn't watch cartoons. He shaved his head with a machete. He looked askance at himself in the mirror. Vietnam troubled him. Indiana and traffic and nicotine fits troubled him. But he was happy. But he was sad. He was the saddest asshole in Amityville.

"The dark hole of meaning punctuates The Unobtainable like a misplaced comma splice." Britney Spears-Mahmood, Interview with Kalypso Shadrach, *The Red Sky at Morning Show* (2040).

Cyberspace as a dead matrix, a petrified vacuum. A burnt waffle of nothingness. "Cyberspace is indeed an enclave of a new sort, a subjectivity which is objective and which, like Luhmann's systems theory, but also like the structuralism and poststructuralism which preceded it, once more does away with the 'centered subject' and proliferates in new, post-individualistic ways." Frederic Jameson, *Archeologies of the Future* (2005). Consider swapping this passage with an excerpt from the Fat Boys' song "All You Can Eat."

Shot of sphenpalatine ganglioneuralgia (trans. margarita brain-freeze)... Steam rises from a soft blue swimming pool at night on the bubbled roof of a spacescraper in 2022 Los Angeles, *Kalifornia* (1993; ref. Brad Pitt's best performance). White tables surround the pool. Aesthetes in bikini briefs sit there and eat the Finger Food of Astronauts.

"Not on Morality, but on Cookery, let us build our stronghold: there brandishing our frying pan, as censer, let us offer sweet incense to the Devil, and live at ease on the fat things *he* has provided for his Elect!" Thomas Carlyle, *Sartor Resartus* (1830-31).

—this is an exegesis of the dreamworld of a narratological Scylla and Charybdis. Failure to adequately perform, process and interpret this exegesis may result in green sunsets and inchoate port-a-potties. Don't wait for the lawyers to sort things out. You can't sue a port-a-potty. Smiles, on the other hand, are a different story...I decided to take my smile to court. "I didn't authorize the smile," I told the judge. "I'm a sad, sad person. Why would I smile?" My smile's attorney guffawed. "That's entirely beside the point, your honor," she said. "Remand." "Remand!" I shouted. My attorney punched me as hard as he could. "Your honor," he said, "remand is an insult. A crime has been committed. If it pleases the court, the prosecution asks that the Accused be imprisoned without bail until such a time that—" "That's enough, counselors," interrupted the judge. A smile overwhelmed his face. He stared down at it in disbelief...One thing always leads to another but cause and effekt are altogether divergent, not to mention endangered, species...To make a fist and not swing it. To drown in a puddle of True Romance. TRACKING SHOT across an obsidian black ocean. The sky overhead is the color of Spectravision, tuned to a dead mammal...A blast of radio static interrupts the narrative..."OK we're back, folks. Give a big round of applause for our first guest, some asshole nobody knows! [Clap track.] He's a certified tool-and-dye maker, a Republikan, and he loves his momma." Two lawyers fly across the stage on wires. They crash into each other, wrestle in the air, then fall into a trap door. [Laff track.]...Memoir = my memory? And yet everybody shits their pants when it ends up being false, or extrapolated, or perverted, or tweaked, or all of the above. Memory is a devious engine. Memory is as trustworthy as a car salesman at a Naïveté Convention. (Ref. name for an upcoming novel: *The Devious Engine*.)...Oasis of Parisian arcades—in his freeze-frame baroque, Walter Benjamin employed the arcades in an attempt to capture/represent the unconscious, more-irreal-than-irreal federation of the human condiment. But the Nazis got him before he could finish. They reach into the potbelly of history and into the fumes of the future and get everyone...Trans. *yarbles*...There are over 60,000 miles of veins and capillaries in the human body. There are less than [???] words in the human mind..."And is that smile sitting in the courtroom today?" asked the judge's newly appointed counsel. In a stone-faced frenzy, the judge threw himself across the bench. "That's him!" he yelled. "That's the smile!" The smile began to grind...Roger Daltrey. *Tommy* (1975) just isn't as good as I want it to be, but I liked Elton John's giant bloodred Doc Martens...Too fuckin' stupid to get into college? Stick Figure University will accommodate you. Just write us a note with your intent to enroll and we'll put you on the docket. Annual price of admission: $179,999.99 per quarter. Room and board not included, dipshit. Send check or money order to...Nothing lasts forever. Eventually everything falls apart. What we need is stronger glue...organic whale fins erupt from the soil of the Amerikan desert...Don't count sheep jumping over fences to fall asleep. Count Earps. Wyatt Earps. Make sure they have .44 magnums and are trigger-happy. Make sure they haven't eaten a decent meal in a week or two. Make sure the fences they try to jump over are too high, and barbed, and electric, and monofilamental. Take no mercy on the Earps. I promise you'll be fast asleep before their mangled corpses pile up to the stars...A magician pulls an inflamed lung out of his hat, tosses it over the audience and shoots it like a skeet. He misses. The lung falls into the lap of a prominent local dignitary. His wife covers her mouth and points and screams and the magician runs offstage and everybody goes apeshit and the lights go flickerflickerflicker...quiet, igneous seashore..................In the end, the lawyers eat everything with a smile. I should have taken the LSATS. What we need are more smiling lawyers—

[Quote here from a credible, authentic source (next blurb is counterfeit, too). Something about the origin of magic. Or lungs. What did James Merrick's doktor/benefactor think about lungs?]

To spend most of one's time waiting for comic book superheroes to transform from everymen into their respective Unleashed Ids, Doppelgängers, Chaosophreaks, etc. Everything leading up to those transformations can be equated with contravened attempts at masturbation in below zero weather. Post-transformation ain't much better. These overmen, and the special effekts used to represent them, promise impossible feats of strength, discourse, violence, agency, etc. But the promise always fails, i.e., one never leaves a Moth(ra) Man with an empty stomach. Hence a revision of my former claim: To leave a Moth(ra) Man with a *deflated* stomach so that one can fully enjoy the scenic chairlift to the next meal.

"I want to take this opportunity to cite [...], who, appropriating the language of [...], who himself tweaked and refined the patois of [...], claimed that [...] misquoted the [...] who uttered the original Nadsat soliloquy that [...] articulated before realizing that the dictionary of Nadsat he had downloaded into his lexicon had been tampered with, i.e., somebody had mixed and matched the definitions in such a way that most of them did not correspond with their lawful terms (e.g. *viddy* = *to talk*, i.e., *govoreet*, instead of *to see*). Hence [...]'s discourse was bezoomny and full of cal. Nonetheless somehow he succeeded in conveying a message that was not only valid and sensible but utterly ethnomethodological, as it were. In any event, [...] writes: '...' (498). Afterwards there was a fist fight." Anonymous Pre-AR Document Recovered from the Third Basement under the Tomb of [...] in Père-Lachaise Cemetery.

"At the end of time, a moment will come when just one man remains. Then the moment will pass. Man will be gone. There will be nothing to show that we were ever here...but stardust. The last man, alone with God...Am I that man?" Capt. Pinbacker, perf. Mark Strong, *Sunshine* (2007). Silhouette of a dark, disintegrating stick figure set against a cosmic wall of fire...Ref. Sgt. Pinback in *Dark Star* (1974).

"What's her name? Linnea. Tell that chick to get naked. All the way. I wanna see bush." Dan O'Bannon, set of *The Return of the Living Dead* (1985).

"Portrait of ultraviolence..." (0.000000037 AR).

"The psychophysical process of attack is not a fundament of this physio-nietzschean martial art. Nor is the art of defense. The enlightened scikungfi fighter will have transcended these useless tactics. Neither *aggression* nor *protection* informs her character. Or rather, these things inform her character to such a degree that they meta-entropically implode into nothingness. I stand here. I blink, I breathe. I exist. And I fucking kill you and eat your gore. That is the True Way of scikungfi. Many like to think they follow and practice the True Way. But the mass man is nothing but a hack bodhisattva. He always will be." Dr Shirley Mai-Pong Gak, Blackbelt, *Tao of Scikungfi, 8th Ed.* (circa Ticky Tacky 2.56 AR).

"Making something new is merely the process of disguising something old in a seemingly creative way. The disguise is the thing—not the thing itself." D. Harlan Wilson, *Dr Identity, or, Farewell to Plaquedemia* (2007).

(NOTE: Faulker did the same shit in "The Bear." See the third chapter. High modernist mxyzptlk. The stuff of *artistes* who fork over everlasting viscera to pursue MFA degrees rather than mxyzptlking their own hackneyed BwOs.)

"010101010001001001001010100010111110101010110011010101010110101
00110110101010101010101010110101010101010101001010101010101010101101
00011010100010101010101110110010101101010101011010101001010101010
10101011101010101000100100100101010001011111010101011001101010101
01011010100110110101010101010101010110101010101010101001010101010101
01010110100011010100010101010101011101100101011010101010101011010101
00101010101010010101010001001001001010100010111110101010101011001
101010101101010011011010101010101010101011010101010101010100101010
1010101010110100011010100010101010101110110010101101010101010110
10101001010101010101110101010100010010010010101000100111110101

0101100110101010110101001101101010101010101010101101010101010101
0010101010101010101011010001101010001010101010111011001010 11010
1010101101010100101010101010010101010101010101111010101010101010
1010101101011101011010111101010101011101011010010010100010010010
0101010001011111010101011001101010101011010100110110101010101010
1010110101010101010101001010101010101010101101000110101000101 0101
010111011002671010110101010101011010101001010101010101011101010101
0001001001001010100010111110101010101100110101010101101010100110110
10101010101010101101010101010101010010101010101010101011010001101
010001010101010111011001010110101010101011010101001010101010100
1010101000100100100101010001011111010101010110011010101010110 1010
0110110101010101010101011010101010101010100101010101010101011010
0011010100010101010101110110010101101010101011010101001010101 01
01010111010101010001001001001010100010111110101010101100110 1010
1011010100110110101010101010101011010101010101010100101010101010
10101101000110101000101010101011101100101011010101010101 10101010
010101010101010110111." Binary Code

The Said vs. the Unsaid.

Vs.

"Usurper." James Joyce, *Ulysses* (1922). Is this grand narrational shiznitosnits-vansamson any different than Snoop Doggy Dogg's 1993 album *Doggy Style*? Equal measures of micturation, excretion, gangstaism and verbomania communicated with equal measures of True Grit.

Cluster of biological salesmen. "AMAZING 2 YEAR GUARANTEE: If you need to start over for any reason we will replace both water-purifier and Sea-Monkey® egg pouches (worth $6.00) plus a free copy of the original. It's fun to raise pet Sea-Monkeys®. Official Sea-Monkey® handbook. A $3.00 value. Free! To enter a claim, send us $3.00 for processing and a stamped, self-addressed envelope to: Sea-Monkey Guarantee, PO Box 809, Bryans Road, MD 20616-0809." Back of Sea-Monkey® Magic Castle Box.

"Expression is not developed through the practice of form, yet form is a *part* of expression. The greater (expression) is not found in the lesser (expression) but the lesser is found within the greater. Having 'no form,' then, does not mean having no 'form.' Having 'no form' evolves from having form. 'No form' is the higher, individual expression....A Jeet Kune Do man faces reality and not crystallization of form. The tool is a tool of formless form." Bruce Lee, *Tao of Jeet Kune Do* (1975). To inject Lee's *raison d'être* (and corporeal physique) into the corpse of literature itself.

"iFFFFPFP."[15] Proto-Indo-European, Obersalzberg (4,000 BC).

Top 100 science fiction clichés:...45) anthropologic aliens; 46) protagonists who manifest as Jesus; 47) antagonists who manifest as Hitler; 48) arch-antagonists who manifest as Teufelsdröckhian failed gourmevangelists and pull the strings of antagonists who manifest as Hitler/John Keats/*Daikaiju*; 49) black holes with speaking voices; 50) intelligent women with immeasurable breasts; 51) first sentences or voice-overs that begin with the phrase: "In an uncompromising future"; 52) infinite stor(i)es of ammunition; 53) endless fucking geekspeak...

"There are no landscapes; there are only selves expressing experiential spaces, and the weird, not the normal, constitutes their true vocabulary." Darin Bradley, "The Self-Weird World: Problems of Being as the Fantastic Invasion in Small Press Speculative Fiction," *Journal of the Fantastic in the Arts* (2007).

"Every word...becomes a spear turned against the speaker. Most especially a remark like this. And so ad infinitum. The only consolation would be: it

15    See note 4.

happens whether you like it or no. And what you like is of infinitesimally little help. More than consolation is: You too have weapons." Franz Kafka, trans. Willa and Edwin Muir, Final Diary Entry (1923).

To come to terms with the phrase "in terms of." Mediation as a form of crapola. So...connect the dots. Compress the Kevin Bacons from Six to Double Negative Infinity Zero Degrees of Meaning...

"Trying to trace the origin of this idea one must assume some misunderstanding of the symbolic meaning of the act of defecation, namely that he who entered into a special relationship with divine rays as I have is to a certain extent entitled to shit on all the world." Daniel Paul Schreber, trans. Ida Macalpine, *Memoirs of My Nervous Illness* (1901).

"...City of Ur..." Gilles Deleuze & Felix Guattari, trans. Robert Hurley, Mark Seem and Helen R. Lane, "The Urstaat," *Anti-Oedipus: Capitalism and Schizophrenia* (1972). Arcologies against the green vastness. Futurespeak. Cold coffee in an expensive shot glass. Timelapse of storm clouds...

"Not wholly as a Spectre does Teufelsdröckh now storm through the world; at worst as a spectre-fighting Man, nay who will one day be a Spectre-queller. If pilgriming restlessly to so many 'Saints' Wells,' and ever without quenching of his thirst, he nevertheless finds little secular wells, whereby from time to time some alleviation is ministered. In a word, he is now, if not ceasing, yet intermitting to 'eat his own heart'; and clutches round him outwardly on the NOT-ME for wholesomer food. Does not the following glimpse exhibit him in a much more natural state?" Thomas Carlyle, *Sartor Resartus* (1830-31).[16]

---

16    Unless specified otherwise, passages originally written in French, German and Nadsat have been translated by Stanley Ashenbach.

# 32
## Houses of If II: The Sequel

Chapter 08 happens again exactly as it happened the first time with one small difference: instead of Styx's "Mr Roboto," they played Mr Mister's "Broken Wings"...

# 33
## Elevator Pitch

Imagine these words rolling across the page in green clock/radio blips. Behind the words, unrelated sepia-toned action sequences...

Get a bunch of dipshits to live in the same hellhole and provide them with a series of insignificant competitions to keep their minds off the certainty of death. Shoot footage for two months. Insert a lifelike mannequin with hair and clothes and everything and see how people react; nail its feet to the floorboards in the living room so nobody steals it. Shoot footage for six months. Zombify the mannequin and equip it with sentience and superhuman strength. Shoot footage until everybody dies. FADE OUT. Image of a scuba diver machinegunning sharks in a filmosophic aquarium surrounded by thousands of idle spectators. A softcore sex scene; the woman wears gaudy lingerie and hasn't shaved her armpits. FADE IN on the mannequin standing on a street corner in futuristic Prague. The mannequin is much taller than the faceless pedestrians that course beneath it. One man, however, about the same height as the mannequin, stops abruptly, circles it a few times, and looks into its eyes. He places a hand on the mannequin's chest in search of a heartbeat. The wind gets loud, louder...SHRIEK-CUT TO a long-range shot of Alaskan tundra. Tall, thin city on the horizon. Shoot footage indefinitely. At some point the silhouette of a man trudges onscreen. We can hear his scarves and coattails flap in the wind. He makes it halfway across the screen and falls down. FIN.

If this doesn't work, resort to the plot of every single episode of *The Incredible Hulk* (1978-82): protag hitchhikes into small redneck town, smalltown rednecks fuck with protag, protag turns green and beats up smalltown rednecks in slow motion, protag hitchhikes out of small redneck town...

If this doesn't work, diverge from machinic plots containing changelings and focus on static bodies, i.e., do an Amerikan pastoral featuring an everyman who can change into the city of Kyoto but maintains an anthropomorphous endoskeleton from beginning to...

...scene in which two gentlemen discuss whether or not their peer is a human or an android. "The only way to tell is to cut him open," says Gentleman #1. Gentleman #2 agrees. They cut Gentleman #3 in half with a chainsaw and he bleeds paper drink umbrellas. "He's human," says Gentleman #2. "Only androids bleed real-looking blood." Gentleman #1 says, "Oh no. We are guilty of murder." They study the severed halves of their peer. "Let's just tell the jury it happened on TV," says Gentleman #1. Gentleman #2 agrees...

# 42
## Houses of If III: The Interquel
## (a.k.a. Revenge of the Scikungfighter)

Prague paid for another ride on the time machine and took it to the end of chapter 08. He accepted a box of cigarettes from Cdre Rabelais, punched Cdre Rabelais, and set the time machine's controls for the end of chapter 17. He went too far and ended up back in chapter 32, where he exacted revenge on Armand Dorleac and Doktor Ray B Flechsig by way of prehistorically cruel and unusual acts of disembowelment. At last he reached his destination, six paragraphs from the end of chapter 17.

...“Ekphrasis!” said Codename Prague. He stormed down the aisle...

...“I know the difference,” snapped the doktor. “Difference is the payload of identity...”

# 44B
## *Daikaiju* Blues in the Bruce Lee Funpark

CNP = Codename Prague. BL = Bruce Lee. TSM = The Sans Merci a.k.a. the Hitler/ Keats Hybrid + *Daikaiju* Monster. DK = *Daikaiju*. And = &. Etc. = etc. Etc....

Somebody cut off CNP's hand as he exited the back door of the theater. A stale martini gushed into the alleyway. He made a pit stop at the Hotel Prague. In the Galactic Pot-Healer Suite, Mädchen "The Prague" Prague and her brother Henrí waited for him, arm in arm. He punched them out. He retrieved a replacement mitt from the briefcase & the mitt welded itself to his wrist. He took off his clothes & put on the trendiest organic exoskeleton in the closet. He drank half a glass of water, handcuffed himself to the briefcase, & left.

"Herr Amboßmann," wheezed "The Prague," groping for him...

On the sidewalk in front of the Hotel Prague a doorman had either been strangled or trampled by a passerby. "There are no marks on his neck," observed one of several bystanders who had gathered around the victim. "And yet there he lays, gasping for breath."

Another bystander said, "Note how, at the same time, he clutches various sectors of his person, which indicates that those sectors may have been accosted by shoes, boots, or what have you."

"Where'd he go?" said CNP, out of breath.

"He's lying right here on the sidewalk." The bystander motioned at the doorman.

"No. The fella did this to him. What direction did he go in? The monster, I mean."

"Jean-Claude Van Damme?"

A paperback novel struck CNP in the the head. "*Weichling!*" shouted TSM from halfway down the block. The monster ran away.

Dazed, CNP pushed the bystanders aside. He tripped over the doorman & stumbled into the street. He fell down. He narrowly escaped the path of a mastodonic streetsweeper, rolling to the other side of the street into the gutter. He got up. Looked around. Traffic. Strobe lights. Cranes. People pointing at him.

No sign of TSM.

He used a nosedove to pick up the monster's scent. He salvaged the novel & let the nosedove sniff it.

"What's it smell like?" asked a bystander.

"Don't ask rhetorical questions," replied CNP & slipped on chrome goggles. He applied the nosedove. It became one with his face, sprouted a set of florid white wings, & lifted him off the ground.

Lips pursed, the nosedove fluttered like a hummingbird & ferried him up & down streets & alleyways & fire escapes at a deafening speed & the city became a corridor of lighting into which he plunged the city pressed down on him he felt like it might collapse dream city dreams of the future nocturnal eidetic *voyages extraordinaires* spatiotemporal techniques illuminated by magic lanterns séances brain-rattling ribbons of spleen façade snapshot-snapshot the corpuscle inhales crepuscular cultureofkaleidoscopicfringe...

Consciousness returned to him hovering over a slingpad. He disengaged the nosedove. Its wings stopped flapping & it slid from his face like an egg.

CNP hit the ground in mid-stride. As always, he cut in line. A few wilburies nursed wounds.

The flight attendant's arm had been dislocated, wrapped around the back of his neck like a stick of tinfoil. He continued to work, though, using his good arm to operate the machine.

"Patience is a verdict," said the flight attendant disapprovingly.

CNP poked him in the chest. "Cut the shit, Johnnycake. Who knocked your block off?"

He pointed at the night sky.

"Where'd he go?"

An overweight new arrival missed a pillow & greased the concrete. The flight attendant sneezed. "He's a man of the crowd. Where do all men of the crowd go? China. *Hong Kong*."

A shiver accompanied CNP's blunt grin...

"He's the type & genius of deep crime," said the flight attendant as a tranzbubble formed on the launching pad. "He refuses to be alone. It will be in vain to follow. You will learn no more of him. Nor of his deeds."

"Fill that thing up with rail scotch. I need a good hangover to even me out. Let's not forget my briefcase." He uncuffed himself & fed the briefcase to the tranzbubble.

Halfway over Khazikstan-22, CNP snorted awake & called the main office. The images of CR & AW sprayed onto a gel-screen. They sat in an empty white room behind a black fold-out table in oversized, overstarched UMUs. Pointless SAMSAs flanked either side of the table. CR & AW looked simultaneously irate & anesthetized. Whatever the case, they had been awaiting his call.

"Mom. Sis," said CNP.

"Not funny enough," said AW.

"Horseshit, Administrator Wichita. I'm all kinds of funny."

CR said, "Where have you been?"

CNP said, "You know where I've been."

CR said, "We want to hear where you think you've been. & what you've done."

"That's what we'd like to know," added AW.

"I've done what I've been told, Commodore Rabelais," said CNP, eyeballing AW. "I always do what I'm told. I'm a robot." He made robot motions with his arms.

"Sixth law of robotics: don't be a pain in the ass," said AW.

"That's the eighth law of robotics," said CNP. "The sixth has to do with empathic synchronicity."

CR said, "Get to the point, Anvil-in-Chief Prague. You called us. We assume you have something worthwhile to tell us. Not to mention you called collect. The MAP is paying for your boloney. Per usual."

CNP stared blankly at the officials.........AW said, "You are a disgrace to—"

"I'm on the trail of this asshole I found in Prague," interrupted CNP. "He committed an illegal act of ekphrasis. He's a monster. I'm chasing the fucker to Hong Kong. I know a smooth criminal when I see one."

AW & CR glanced at one another. "Ekphrasis?" mouthed AW.

CR looked at CNP. "So you're no longer in Prague, then?"

"I'm no longer in Prague. That's correct."

"So you've had relations with a certain femme fatale, then?" AW & CR snickered under their breath.

"Relations? Grow up, Farmer Ted."

"So you've completed your mission, then?"

"No. Yes. Maybe. Take your pick. I never knew what the mission was."

"That's beside the point," said CR. "The less you know about your mission, the better. You shouldn't even know that you're on a mission. How do you know that?"

"Maybe he is a robot, after all," said AW.

"Who?" said CR.

AW pointed at CNP through the gel-screen.

CR frowned. "Who's that? I don't know who that is. How did you get this number? The MAP fines prank callers, without mercy, & at the outer limits of absurdity. I hereby fine you the head of Alfredo Garcia."

"Failure to produce this head in a timely manner with period-piece sunglasses intact," interjected AW, "will result in All Out Conversion to Suicidal

Gore wherein you will be forced to stab yourself to death with Peckinpahesque recklessness & whimsy."

Smiling, CNP said, "At any rate, *zèng bié*. I'll let you know how everything pans out. Or not. I do what I want. That's all a man can do. You know what they say, boys. The early bird catches the mutated bullfrog. Someone let the cat out of the black hole. Go fly a kakistocracy. Keep your irons in the fires of Eden. A woman's work is never overcooked. Beauty is only a skin rash. Look before you lionize. There is no honor among thespians. Walls have frontal lobes. Ignorance is piss. Great minds think alone. No news is good news with Gary Gnu..."

CNP told the tranzbubble to give him his briefcase. He re-cuffed himself to it.

The tranzbubble said thank you & evaporated...

Panoramic shot of Kowloon beneath a pink sun:...terminal sprawl of mirrored matted blinking bottlenecks turtlenecks torpedoes cacti antennae scratch the sss-Ur-[f](ace) of atmosphere behind it the ancient sloping backbone of a mountain green as a special effekts superscreen...Tronlike grid of bleeding pseudofolliculitis streets & (a)causeways the silver chutes penetrate the hot depths in orderly alloyed oiled brigades of tendrils... fireballs spewed from eyes/holes in the sky...& the scikungfi fights broke out like hives in bullet-time CGI...contact dermatitis breakout/breakthrough... Hot-tempered ichi/alpha males clad in flashy Judogis & Keikogis & Aikidogis & Doboks & Shinobi Shozukus & Cobra Kahn uniforms clashed *en bloc* in the clouds & on rooftops & on the streets with fists & feet & trans-tech WMIs (Weapons of Mass Instruction) vibroswords flowswords blowswords chainswords bioswords hyperswords nietzscheswords swords that altogether defied swordlike behavior...steady thunder of dares threats soporific warcries...

Vertigo.

For a moment, CNP merged with the spectacle of sociometroscikungfidom—the technology of Desire extended into its eschatological occupation, penetrating it, aluminizing it, metamorphosing it...& suddenly he had lost himself, body & mind, in a fit of passive-aggressive ecstasy. He was no longer a man. He was Abba. He was the city.

*Verfremsdungseffekt.*

As quickly as he had lost himself, he reestablished a sense of personhood. He was not the city. He was not Abba. He was just a man. He forced himself to say it out loud. "I am not Abba. I am not Abba. I am—"

A pillow swallowed CNP like a hungry mollusk.

CHASE SCENE: CNP pursued TSM on foot, then by fanglider, jetpack, & batsuit. TSM hurled taunts & Molotov cocktails over its shoulder. They hailed wicker ferries that took them to Hong Kong where DKs demolished skyscrapers & devoured innocent antagonists by the handful. Long sequence here with a vivid synesthesic depiction of Hong Kong's Tetsuo Sektor.

Cornered & out of breath, TSM did the only thing it could do: took a bus to the Bruce Lee Funpark...

DREAM: The astro-zombie evolved into a man who possessed a community college associates degree. He stumbled across the lawn & tripped over a piece of yard art. Died. A portal to a ridiculous science fictional dimension masquerading as a Pop-Up Video bubble formed over his skull. Inside the bubble was the author photo of an extra-terrestrial alien, sharp white chin resting on the back of a loose fist.

Over the megascape of dragoncoasters, an echoic aluminum screech...

LOCATION: Chopsocky Sektor, Hong Kong, China. SIZE: 1 Sq. Mile. POPULATION: 80,000 *daikaijus*, 10,000 Bruce Lees, 5 Chuck Norrises, 1 James Coburn & half a Kareem Abdul-Jabbar. COST OF ADMISSION: Death Wish + Tier Eight Knowledge of Jeet Kune Do, Wuxia Pian & Postspeculative Scikungfi. FEATURED RIDE:...FEATURED SNACK FOOD: Bamboo Surprise...

CNP uncuffed himself from the briefcase. A DK hawked a fireball at him. He dodged it & recuffed himself to the briefcase.

The Bruce Lee Funpark upheld tight security measures, its inhabitants permanently on the brink of leaking out & infesting wider Hong Kong & the Chinese mainland. It had happened before. At one point the Chinese government was being run entirely by BL & DK life forms—senate scikungfi fights from that era appeared in syndication to this day—prompting surrounding countries (e.g. Mongolia, Vietnam, North Korea, Russia, etc.) to install various Bruce Li[17] androids & *Supa Robottos* in powerful administrative positions so as to at least contend with the infection on a sociopolitical level. Aided by the council of several notable Amerikan pulp science fiction paperbacks, however, Chinese natives were able to quell the infection, & now every BL & DK had been neutered, as it were, so that if an aspirant scalawag stepped beyond the clearly demarcated boundaries of the BLF, it vaporized. As an additional precaution, the BLF boasted thousands of vigilant, oscillating tower canons. Sometimes the tower canons killed indiscriminately, without provocation. Sometimes they killed innocent, paying customers. But as with all postreal places & spaces, one always pays, enters & exists at one's own risk.

..."Catch me if you can," said TSM & disappeared into a game room. CNP

---

17      Screen name of BL impersonator Ho Chung Tao, who also worked as a stuntman under the pseudonym James Ho. Weary of production constraints to replicate BL at every turn, Li gave up acting in the early 1980s after a run of over thirty films. He owned and operated a Taiwanese gymnasium for years afterwards prior to his accidental death by rogue throwing star. For more on his biography, refer to Elmore Petite's *Three Bruces in a Pod: The Interstitial Abductions of B. Springsteen, B. Campbell, and B. Li.*

chased the monster inside.

The game room was full of old coin-operated arcade machines—row after row of Konami® Kung Fu interrupted by the odd game of Contra, Track & Field, & Tutankham. A BL hunched over each machine manipulating ball-peen joysticks & fingering red buttons.

CNP advanced up & down the aisles. He called out to TSM, insulting the monster's manhood & sense of style, ensuring the monster of immanent demolition, but CNP's attention mainly fell on the wide assortment of BLs that populated the arcade, all of whom swore in Chinese & made irritated, high-pitched BL noises as they lost their respective games & had to stuff more quarters into the machines' slots.

There were BLs in black tights.

There were BLs in parachute pants.

There were BLs in yellow *Kill Bill* uniforms.

There were BLs with big hair, BLs with butt cuts & buzz cuts, BLs with mullets & Mohawks & Jheri curls.

There were Cato BLs.

There were cartoon BLs.

There were Mr Hyde BLs, Frankenstein BLs, Nosferatu BLs, Wolfman BLs, Lizardman BLs, Invisible Man BLs, Planet of the Apes BLs, Caliban BLs, street mime BLs, Jason Vorhees BLs, Mecha-BLs (*in effigie* Cylons, Voltron, Megatron, Biotron, Mr Roboto, Robocop, the Tin Man, the Maria-Robot, Gort, Herbie the Volkswagon, Dr Identity, Yul Brynner, Lance Henriksen, F451's Mechanical Hound, etc.), Adam Ant BLs, Grendel BLs, Sasquatch BLs, Medusa BLs, Jack the Ripper BLs, Morlock BLs, Oscar the Grouch BLs, Mugwump BLs, Incredible Hulk BLs, Clockwork Orange BLs, Lady Chatterly BLs, Jackie Chan BLs, Pokémon BLs, Teletubby BLs...

There were DK-sized BLs who reposed on their knees & Lilliputian BLs who stood on each other's shoulders like totem poles.

There were scrawny BLs from the early years. There were shredded, musclebound BLs from the last days.

BLs with rubber noses.

BLs with Doc Oc tentacles and Ultimate Warrior facepaint.

BLs whose six-packs had virally overtaken the rest of their bodies, rendering them giant washboard six-packs crowned by dark, pubic ruffs of hair.

BLs overeasy, BLs à la carte, Blaxploitation BLs, Bruceploitation BLs, BLs [Mad Lib]...

The VG protagonist of a Solomon Grundy BL playing Contra ran out of ammo & an enemy soldier shot him dead. It was the last man. The BL threw a temper tantrum; it was supposed to have unlimited ammo. It slammed a fist into the screen, shattering it, then punched the arcade game with right & left hooks & hammer fists. Soon the machine lay in smoking, sparking chunks. Unsatisfied, the BL stomped on the wreckage. Nearby BLs told him to grow up. The Solomon Grundy BL turned its aggression on them & a fight broke out.

The BLs stopped fighting when they noticed CNP watching them.

"Solomon Grundy BL, born on a Monday as well." The android gnashed its teeth. "Ticket please." It stuck out its hand.

CNP blinked. "Ticket?"

All of the BLs in the arcade turned from their games & looked at CNP expectantly. Sound of VG protagonists being killed or trounced by their opponents...

"Grundy BL crush pimple-man!"

CNP touched his face. "I don't have any pimples."

50+ BLs blitzed CNP...scikungfi battle royal...they flowed out of the arcade into the BFL proper...The scene went BLACK & RED. Coronets warmed up. Drum roll on a splash cymbal...West Side Story finger-snapping sequence in silhouette. A Pony Boy BL in tight blue jeans & a wifebeater led the family of scikungfi fighters across the stage of concrete & asphalt & iron.....................................

CNP grabbed the faces of the BLs & smashed them into the ground & their heads exploded like water balloons. He darted up the leg & the torso of a DK & ripped its beak in two & the movie monster's throat turned inside out &

its tongue went stiff with rigor mortis. He killed eight more DKs in the same manner. BLs clutched their hairdos. BLs made sharp exhaling noises.

Flickering lights. A headache brought on by a surge of inclement weather.

NARRATIVE MALFUNCTION...circuits overlarded........................................
....................................................................................................................
.................................................................. Review of this sentence in *The Prague Daily*: "This sentence is full of little dots. This sentence is full of *itself*. & its author has merged with Dr Oblivion. A cancerous sentence. An evil, indecipherable sentence. *Introibo ad altare Dei*...P.S. the word 'overloaded' is misspelled..."

TSM hid behind a wall & clubbed CNP with a metal pipe when he ran by, nearly decapitating him. CNP tore off his damaged head & threw it aside. Martini juice ejaculated from the neck wound. He uncuffed himself from the briefcase, removed a fresh head, put it on, & recuffed himself to the briefcase. He shook a finger at TSM & flicked his nose with a thumb.

TSM vanished into a herd of DKs...

### Random Chapter w/in Chapter: There Is a Fifty-Foot Mecha-Michael Ironside Monster Crawling Out of a Hole...

Some actors always play hard bastards, but they are often not hard bastards in "real life." Family members and intimate acquaintances compare them to figures the likes of teddy bears, pacifists, "gentle giants" or "big sweeties."

This is not the case with Canadian-born actor Michael Ironside (1950-2056) a.k.a. Frederick Reginald "They Sucked Their Brains Out" Ironside.

During adulthood, Ironside was documented on multiple occasions exhibiting behavior in "real life" evocative of hard bastardry. The cause of his death at the age of 106 remains a mystery. After considerable debate, coroners finally validated the COD with one simple word: **ANGER.**

Ironside's family donated his corpse to the Ministry of Applied Pressure, as specified in his will. The MAP, then, in stride with the era's dominant fashion craze, extracted the late celebrity's DNA & used it to manufacture a legion of fifty-foot tall mecha-Michael Ironside monsters, the purpose of which was never made public, although it has been speculated that an extremist faction of the Department of Goodwill & Selflessness intended to use them against an extremist faction of the Department of Unexplainable Metaphysical Occurrences that threatened to stab holes in the fabric of reality so as to deflate reality like a car tire. The threat never came to fruition; in retrospect, people think of it as an urban legend, despite the many fifty-foot mecha-Michael Ironside monster sightings that have transpired since the actor's death. At the moment, for instance, outside the front door of Prague's Goltz-Kinsky Palace, there is a fifty-foot mecha-Michael Ironside monster crawling out of a hole...

## Deliberate Chapter w/in Chapter w/in Chapter:...
## & Out of Another Hole...

...crawls a 100-foot Powers Boothe zombie wearing a 5,000 gallon hat. He stomps on the Ironside monster & dares the motherfucking shiteater to...

TSM metamorphosed into a DK. Its uniform burst into shreds as it inflated & changed color & grew scales fangs claws & contracted an oviparous physiology... The result stood higher than the BLF's tallest Ferris wheel. Like the acorn from which it sprouted, it was a crossbreed. The stegosaural spikes that ran the length of its spine reminisced Godzilla, but it lacked a tail in favor of Krakenesque tentacles and Cloverlike external esophagi, & it possessed the head of a Howdy Doody ventriloquist doll with round Mothraic eyes & a long Rodanian beak.

Dragoncoasters corkscrewed overhead, emitting signature BL grunts, squawks & hiyaaaas!

The TSM→DK howled when it reached full size and saw CNP. Metamorphic steam hissed from between the cracks of its scales.

The tides turned, and the Chased became the Chaser...

### Preclimax

A BL screamed & his face melted. A BL screamed & his head exploded. A BL screamed & the fruit salad of his innards exited his body from infinite unchoreographed serrations.

...rather than crush CNP in his fist, the TSM→DK decided to eat him, chewing only hard enough to break a few bones & leaving the rest to the acid pool of its stomach. CNP countered the move with his briefcase, which he rammed into the TSM→DK's mouth. The briefcase expanded into a surfboard and pierced the TSM→DK's chin. The monster shrieked in pain... and shrunk...

CNP fell from the TSM→DK's grasp onto a waterslide at the bottom of which BLs & DKs awaited him. An additional/extended scikungfi fight unfolded.

## Climax

They fired a Double-H (Heinlein + Hubbard) bomb at CNP from the crow's nest of a Sky Swat. A silent, B&W mushroom cloud of canned hypermasculinity knocked him off his feet & threw him into a chickenwire fence, but he was man enough to survive the ordeal, & he retaliated as his exoskeleton deionized all traces of radiation, firing a blowforce projectile at the crow's nest from a bazooka. His targets exploded like frogs slung against a brick wall. He turned the bazooka on other targets, i.e., everybody became a target, BLs & DKS & funpark staff alike, & he did flips & 360s & helicopters through the air, blowing shit up, blowing heads & appendages off, demolishing rides & buildings & DKs & tiki bars & french-fry kiosks, & he landed on the irimoya of The Big Boss building, & he cast the bazooka aside & flexed the transanthropoid muscles of his organic exoskeleton as the world beneath him continued to explode & smolder & burn... Smoke cleared in patches & CNP spotted TSM a short distance from his perch. He leapt off the irimoya & descended on the monster in the yellow dusk...

TSM lay on its back, naked, breathless, coughing blood. "This smoke hurts my lungs," it wheezed. "Is this normal smoke or something else? *Scheiße*."

"I think it's normal smoke," said CNP, tearing a steel trashcan from the concrete. "But normal is a relative term. Technology these days. Not to mention different body types react to chemicals in different ways." He pressed the trashcan over his head.

TSM raised a hand & spread out all the fingers. "I'm just a robot," it said.

"I'm just a man," CNP replied.

"Different species."

"One & the same."

The echoic caw of an Arabian Ostrich preceded the smashing of TSM's skull beneath the authorial weight of the trashcan. The assassination was succeeded by a long, Gullyfoylesque speech given to the residue of BLs & DKs in CNP's vicinity as to how they should "learn themselves" to be better hosts & more intellectually-oriented hominids.

## Anticlimax

"Watch this."

He clipped the noodle vendor with a flying kick.

"I have come here to chew bubble gum and kick ass," he said. "And I'm all out of Donkey Kong."[18]

He jammed a stick of Doublemint into his mouth, then hopped over a turnstile & strode towards the ocean...

---

18    "I have come here to chew bubble gum and kick ass. And I'm all out of bubble gum." Rowdy Roddy Piper as Nada, *They Live* (1988). Subsequently Nada blasts a policeman with a "1957 cheese dip" or "formaldehyde" face that he is able to visualize with the aid of special sunglasses. He goes on to blast several other human and non-human inhabitants of the bank in which the scene is set.

# 48
## There Is a Hole Here Where Something Else Used to Be

# 51
## The Resistance of Memory

Cliché-within-a-cliché: a family of boneless clocks hanging from randomly assorted inanimate objects...The sundry spatial vastnesses of Mr Dali's paintings have been associated with the female genitalia by critics as well as by the Catalan artist himself. "It is a vagina," said Mr Dali, pointing a lean finger at the landscape of *The Persistence of Memory*, "and anything that intrudes upon that space"—pointing at a distant stone now—"is a cock. Vaginas describe and rule the diegetic irrealities of my canvases like interstitial neurastheniacs. They expose themselves—nothing more—and the spectrum of war and peace and all that lies in between is relegated to the cult of little men. There is nothing more dangerous than a little man. Remember—"

The Nowhere Man looked like he had gotten into a fight with a cheap sheet of wallpaper. His crinkled cape and hood exhibited a faded mushroom pattern that changed shape and color in synch with his mood. His limbs were thin, sticklike, possibly arthropodal. A black hole had swallowed his face. Sometimes, in certain lights, a discernable human visage emerged from the hole. The visage was all angles, scars, sharp edges—a blotch of glinting razorblades within which pulsed two yellow asterisks.

[The Nowhere Man's appearance on-page is always accompanied by a low, distorted screech that rises in intensity and pitch...]

Lackluster hysteria that goes: "Ha-ha-ha-ha-ha-ha-ha-ha-ha-ha-ha-ha-ha-ha-ha-ha-ha-ha-ha-ha-ha-ha-ha-ha..."

...When Codename Vincent Prague was born, his parents resolved to name him Pail. They told everybody that's what they were going to name him as his mother's stomach inflated like a niggling statistic.

"Pale, like, without color?" inquired family, friends, and strangers.

"Pale does not denote something *without* color," said Father Prague, "but rather something *deficient* in color. But that's not the Pail we mean. We mean the Pail you put things in." To demonstrate, he placed a small object into a receptacle. His audience clapped...

"Father scarred me deeply. See?" Prague peeled off the brown skin of his forehead and exposed the frontal lobe. Sparks rolled across brain tissue in waves...

"Nothing's changed. Being a black man in a meta-pulp science fictional diegesis is no different than being a black man in agrarian Amerika. Even when you're the protagonist. Every day is White Boy Day."

[...mnemonic vestiges of Hitler and Keats overlapped spliced vivisected stitched together...Hitler in the Bunker. Keats on the Death Bed...Close-up on Jean-Claude Van Damme's wen.]

"[Dialogue]," said The Nowhere Man over a crescendo of distortion......

After Reality, mad scientism became a normative condition. It was not limited to whimsical, diabolical and/or compensatory monster making and purple people eating. Simply burning one's toast might be characterized as an instance of mad scientism. In effekt, all AR subjects had, by default, gone insane, and all of them had contracted a certain evil genius and pseudotechnological fetish—viz., everybody became a stock character or a caricature of a stock character in a pulp sci-fi diegesis.

...When Doktor Hermann Teufelsdröckh was born, his parents resolved to name him Doktor. They told everybody that's what they were going to name him as his mother's stomach inflamed like a nacreous welt.

"What if he becomes a doktor when he grows up?" inquired family, friends, and strangers.

"Then he will be a doktor twice over," said Father Teufelsdröckh, "and his identity will be doubly reinforced."

"Actually his 'identity,' per se, will only be *reinforced*," said a Nowhere Man. "The first doktor won't count. Do you understand?"

Remote heat lightning.

They strapped Special Agent Prague into an anti-suicide smock. They realized they had made a mistake and strapped him into a suicide smock. They realized they had made another mistake.

"Do you want me dead or alive?" asked Prague.

"Either way works for us," they replied. "Which is to say, we can't decide."

...the impossibility of memory/history. Hence the impossibility of narrative/identity. Authorial direction. Authorial oppression. The Third Little Pig used barcodes instead of bricks. The result: a house that the Big Bad Wolf tried to purchase for $29.95 in three easy installments...

# 56
## Amerikan Hemorrhage Dictionary of Scikungfi

Hi-def digital pastiche of screaming mouths from Hong Kong action flix (emphasis on Bruce Lee, Sonny Chiba, Kwan Tak Hing and Siu-Lung Leung) interspersed with bits of costumed derring-do and *henshin* (trans. from Japanese "to change or transform the body") wuxia sequences. The last shot belongs to *Inframan* (1975; tagline: "The Man Beyond Bionics") in which protagonist Rayma/Inframan (actor Danny Lee a.k.a. Li Hsiu Hsien) metamorphoses into a *daikaiju* and performs a *tomoe-nage* judo throw on an orange, *daikaiju*-sized Tarantula Man (actor unknown), then hits him with a flying double-punch, then tosses him into an energy plant. The Tarantula Man shrinks. Begin credits. Before we fade out to black, the scene returns and Inframan steps on the Tarantula Man with a giant white boot. Ketchup and mustard spurt from the creature's flattened corpse.

# 1007
## Short Fable

A man's **shadow** elected to cast the man. The **shadow** peeled itself off the street, stretched out its arms, leapt onto the man's shoulders, and stomped him into place. Then the sun went down.

# 1008
## Long Fable

Two people hack off their arms and spray each other with their innards to prove who's more fashionable. They bleed out. A waiter drags them into a reanimation booth...What is the role of Gary, Indiana? To supply citizens with a preview of Hell before the Big Plunge. Sprawling neoindustrial badlands—so ugly they're beautiful. Further down the yella brick road: spatial anxiety...In Gary, Indiana, there are always Beetles' songs in air. I mean the band before they grew long hair and got hooked on chronic and gin and juice...This is the arena in which subjects have wired their bodies to die in creative ways. Death as the end of creativity. Death as the only act of imagination after reality... Penetrate history. The deeper the thrust, the deeper the shit. But there are clearly demarcated signposts. One signpost reads:

**THIS IS THE MOMENT IN TIME WHERE POP AESTHETICS**
**SWALLOWED/DIGESTED/MULCHED/VAPORIZED**
**THE ICONOGRAPHY OF HUMAN**
**RELATIONS/EXISTENCE/LANGUAGE/EXPERIENCE/CONSCIOUSNESS**

Other signposts note the birth of the sandwich, the midlife crisis of a haunted house, the death of Doktor Hermann Teufelsdröchk...Old age means too much memory, too many photo stills and movies crammed onto the un/pre/conscious mind's screen. An old bastard needs to start from scratch, even if he may not want to. Remember the last days of reality? Heads spontaneously exploding on every street corner and rooftop? Celluloid oozed from the neck holes like the Beverly Hillbillies' bubblin' crude...

There is a sculpture of a man with a fist for a head that throws its voice from one knuckle to another. His arms dangle comfortably at his sides. He stands upright. He rises to a height of over 500 feet and houses thousands of tenants. Through the windows of his flesh—the windows that have not been painted black—the attentive viewer may behold a crossword puzzle of strange, muted sex acts. Who is this man?

Ekphrasis. Translation: representation. Translation: something that stands for something else.

Translation: code.

To name a code is to further encode a code. A code needs to be The Unnamable. The disappearance of identity and the self is the first step to decoding the code. The ensuing steps progress in an infinite regression.

Somewhere beyond the spacetime continuum, the actions of one man will contain the code of the postreal, postfuturistic, posthuman condition. That man will not be an everyman. Nor will he be a superman. Nor will the code that his actions contain be the stuff of legend.

# 1111
## Untitled Prague Rejektion Letter (on Marvin the Martian Letterhead)

[Address]

Dear Mr Anvil-in-Chief Vincent "Codename" Prague:

We have spoken to the producers of *Cats* in the
Former Czech Republik and collectively decided to
liquidate your position as Anvil-in-Chief. At your
earliest convenience, please turn in your body to
the nearest MAP way station for processing and (dis)
integration. As of the present moment—i.e. the moment
you lay eyes on this document (i.e. right now)—you
no longer exist. Please do not mistake this abrupt
transition to nonexistence as a figurative reality.
I assure you that it is a literal reality. You are
neither here nor there. We certainly do not know,
acknowledge, or regard you as a person, robot, alien,
black man, or inanimate object. Thus this letter does
not exist because one cannot write something to a
nonexistent person, etc.

On behalf of the MAP, we would like to take this
opportunity to thank you for your service, hard

work, etc. Best of luck to you. Keep in touch!

Yours,

*Ron*

Commodore Ronald Rabelais
General Assistant Managerial Choreographer of Mortal Affairs
Department of Anthropologism
Ministry of Applied Pressure
Klamm Central
Slaughterhouse $#@%?*&!
P.O. Box •
City City, State 83
USAmerika

# 1517
## The Death of Doktor Hermann Teufelsdröchk

"One day—I shall make all the universe wild and primitive! I shall destroy all the civilized planets![19]...Did I say that? Am I the man who said that thing? Or am I just a medium through which some liminal patriarch has articulated his ultimate desire? This makes sense. Nobody says *shall* anymore...But no. I am not a medium. I am a plagiarist. *I am plagiarism incarnate.*"

Dr Teufelsdröchk sprinkled a pinch of garlic salt on his tongue. He closed his mouth. The taste of the garlic salt slowly disappeared into his tongue-flesh as he reflected on and measured the content of his dialogue.

The Ugly and Untruth monsters lifted their guns and blew two holes in Dr Teufelsdröchk's chest.

<<<BE KIND: REWIND>>>

[Another extended description of Dr T's laboratory. Focus on various Spencer's Gifts items (e.g. plasma spheres). Background melody: Freddy Mercury megamix or incidental music from Snoop Doggy Dogg's "Doggy Dogg World." Dr T = Rotwang ~ Loss of Hel + Failure to Become Top Chef. He hunches over a futuristic-looking gas range preparing comfort food. Enter Ugly and Untruth monsters. They startle him. Dress them like the assassins at the end of Kafka's *The Trial*. Ref. the introductory paragraph to the last chapter, "The End": "On the evening before K's thirty-first birthday—it was

---

19    From "Lepus and the Colliding Planets featuring Buzz Crandall of the Space Patrol," by Fletcher Hanks (as Bob Jordan), *Planet Comics*, Issue 7, 1940. Dialogue spoken by a lava-skinned madman known as "Lepus the Fiend" from "his scientific stronghold on an undiscovered star."

about nine o'clock, the time when a hush falls on the streets—two men came to his lodging. In frock coats, pallid and plump, with top hats that were apparently irremovable" (223).]

"Where are my assistants?" said the doktor. He wore an old velvet robe with his initials stitched onto the lapel.

"Are we our brothers' keepers?" said the monsters in unison.

"They're not your brothers, Cain. They're your makers. They're your parents."

"My father was an etc. etc. etc.," said the Untruth monster. "Ergo:—" It ran a palm across its face and produced a vacant expression.

Dr Teufelsdröchk stirred a pan of chopped morels and scallions with a spatula, then added a bowl of shredded [???]. He worked the [???] around the pan...dash of spices...splash of white wine. He took a long sip from the bottle. "Gewürztraminer. Not a bad year. But I can tell that somebody has shit on the grapes. Just a hint of shit, mind you. But I can taste it. Never trust a German grape stomper."

"We have come here to murder you," said the Untruth monster.

"We have come here to murder you," repeated the Ugly monster.

"Where are my assistants?" repeated the doktor.

[Smartassed remark here that rivals the tone of Billy Zane's ultrabourgeois alpha male in *Titanic*.]

Dr Teufelsdröchk turned around. He loosened his robe and exposed himself. "Very well." [Image of Leo DiCaprio whooping at the fore of the ship.] "So my beloved Truth and Beauty have effekted greener pastures. God bless them."

The assistant monsters traded vacant expressions.

[Repeat the first three paragraphs of the chapter.]

"Ah, that hurts me, sirs," said Dr Teufelsdröchk in a detached French accent. "Well. You got me, as they say. There's certainly no question about it. Indeed no." Dull red mud emptied from the wounds in a stream of claymation. He made no effort to plug them. "It's better this way. I am not an old man. But I have never wanted to be an old man. Thank you dearly for fulfilling my wildest desire. Ha!" He looked at his wounds and outlined them with trembling fingers. His robe slipped off his shoulders.

The assistant monsters shot him again. One shot hit him in the navel and his stomach and intestines sprayed out of his back onto the cooking range. The other shot blew off half of his head.

Dr Teufelsdröchk didn't fall down. He sort of marched in place, gesticulating with the spatula and making crude choking noises. An eyeball hung onto his cheek like a dead treefrog. Again and again he tried to push the eyeball back into its socket with his free hand. But the socket wasn't there.

[Continue to describe the gory details of Dr T's murder. The assistant monsters shoot him a few more times. Finally Dr T falls onto the range and catches fire. The fire spreads throughout the kitchen, etc. FINAL *MISE EN SCÈNE*: The assistant monsters exit the smoking entrance of Dr T's "lair," amble across a vast prairie and vanish into a distant bed of sunflowers.]

# -66.799
## The Nowhere Incident

Nobody seemed to know who Vincent Prague was anymore. Nobody had asked him for an autograph in...how long? So long he had almost forgotten his name. He touched his face to make sure he wasn't wearing a mask.

He recalled the incident that made him famous...

[FLASHBACK: Dialogue between CNP and The Nowhere Man (TNM). Prelude to the climactic/originary scikungfi fight in the novel.]

[TNM as a distant relative of Mister Nobody (see pg. 208 of *The DC Comics Encyclopedia*). Explain...TNM has the unique ability to exist nowhere and everywhere at once, i.e., he can project his psyche (nowhere) onto the spatial plane of reality (everywhere)...TNM as a wax figure (see 2nd entry in *Passagenwerk* chapter). Whenever he appears, speaks, etc., there is a dull screeching sound in the background...Show how CNP's preoccupation with the impossibility of the assassination of TNM pathologizes him. He is haunted by TNM's semiotic ghost.]

They discussed the possibility of chess to settle the score. Then they discarded the idea. Both Prague and The Nowhere Man could see thousands of moves into the future. They might be playing for years.

[FIGHT: Each martial artist brandishes a flashy sci-fi weapon, says he doesn't need it, and tosses it aside. They do this for hours before engaging in hand-to-hand combat, which only lasts for half a minute before they revert to weaponry. Long stylized scikungfi battle. At one point TNM dares CNP to fight him with a savage, large-breasted woman slung over his shoulder. He returns the dare. The fight continues...pause. The combatants retire to the bushes. They emerge twenty or so minutes later smoking cigars. Resume fight...Then, unexpectedly, CNP beats TNM via a strong grip on TNM's wrist (ref. *Beowulf*)... How does TNM die?]

[Metanarrational elements. Something about science fiction. Mention Gernsback and/or Campbell?]

[How do I account for the chapter being a negative number?]

[Cram chapter with authorial notes in brackets. And yet keep the chapter under 500 words.]

[End w/anecdotal fragment: "In an alternate diegesis, CNP was a town crier, which is to say, he was the only person in the town who could cry because everybody else's tear ducts had dried out. He stood in the town square, weeping, and the villagers worshipped his false sorrow like a true deity..."]

# Codename Prague

Commodore Rabelais faded onto the screen in monochrome stop-motion animation. He stood in his office with hands folded. Behind him, beside him—the corpses of SAMSAs and janitors.

"*Narrative of the Life of Codename Prague*," he said. "There should have been more sex scenes in this narrative. There was only one, by my reckoning. It was an anal sex scene, and that's a step in the right direction. But it's one measly step."

Gray bolts of static moved up and down the screen. Prague rapped his knuckles against the console. The static disappeared, then came back twice as strong.

"Where the hell are you, Vinnie?" said Rabelais. "I can barely see you."

"You know where I am. I'm in outer space. I'm in a spaceship. Zero gravity, motherfucker." Prague's voice echoed for miles, bouncing down the corridor of the unmanned freighter he had stowed away on. He didn't know where the freighter was going. The nearest black hole, for all he cared. He needed a vacation. A terminal vacation. The Ides of Misanthropy commanded it. He had no hard feelings. Live long enough, and one of two things killed you: cancer or the hatred of mankind.

"I can see that much," replied Rabelais as Prague floated onscreen, offscreen, onscreen, offscreen...

"What's with the dead meat?"

Rabelais peered around the office. He stomped on a body that wouldn't surrender its reflexes. "I ran out of androids. I'm waiting for the MAP to replenish my supply. Sometimes they take awhile. *Elend ist ich*. But it's not the end of the world."

Long pause. Prague floated counterclockwise until he was upside-down in the corridor. Rabelais smirked.

"One day," Prague whispered, "I shall make all the universe wild and primitive. I shall destroy all the civilized planets."[20]

"What? What? I can't hear you."

"I think I deserve an explanation."

"Explanation? I'm afraid you'll have to be more specific, Vinnie. Spell it out for me. Treat me like a child."

"I always do." He closed his eyes, listening to the flow of Victory martini juice through his veins. If only he could afford Hammer blood. Things might have turned out differently...He opened his eyes. "Why did you torture me?"

"Torture you? The MAP tortures everybody, young man. Being employed by the MAP doesn't exempt you from being abused by the MAP. That goes for any legitimate Amerikan bizwax. It's common sense. How long have you been in space? How long have you been alone? Outer space and a lonesome dove—not a good combination."

Prague put a gun to his head. "What was the purpose of my mission?"

"Purpose of your mission? That's none of your business. That's nobody's business. How many times do I have to tell you?"

"Tell me again."

A SAMSA shuffled onscreen. He looked innocently at Prague, then at the stiffs, then at Rabelais. "You, uh, wanted to see me, sir?" he said.

Rabaleis jumped on the SAMSA and strangled him to death, screaming, "Let me strangle you! Let me strangle you! Let me strangle you!" The SAMSA let him.

Rabelais stood and brushed off his suit. He undid his tie and gripped each end. "The purpose of your mission was to send you on a wild goose chase,"

20    See note 19.

he announced. "Period. At the same time, the purpose of your mission was *not* to send you on a wild goose chase, which is to say, your mission was to take certain premeditated actions that resulted in certain inevitable effekts. Either way the mission tells a story. In the end, that's all that matters. That's all people are interested in. Narrative. The fiction of everyday life."

Prague floated rightside-up. He didn't say anything. He pulled the trigger of the gun. *Click...click...click...click...click...*

"Fine. Be that way. Here is another 'explanation.'" Cdre Rabelais paced back and forth, moving between sharp fits of slowtime and fasttime. He produced a kind of sign language that looked like the motions of a marionette puppeteer with his balls in a sling. Then he returned to a position of semi-attention. Static continued to garble the screens on both parties' ends.

"Do you understand now?" said Rabelais.

*...click...click...click...*

The Commodore used thumbs and fingers to make an O-shape through which he peered at Prague with one eye. "What about now?"

*...click...click...*

"Most unfortunate. Well. Let me put it to you this way...It was revealed to the Ministry of Applied Pressure that you possessed a code capable of inciting the next evolutionary stage of postreal mankind. The MAP had been searching for this code for decades. We found it in your toilet one night on a routine check of your feces. We crack open everybody's toilets, every night, and check their feces when they sleep. The code had never appeared in your physiology before. Was it something you ate? Had you been bitten by an alien or a vampire? Had you injected yourself with experimental cleaning products? No matter. There was the code. Now we had to unlock it."

*...click.........click...*

"Based on research performed by some of the top Phildickian minds in the Amerikanized world, we inserted you into carefully prescribed and constructed social and spatial matrices. It was hoped that over time your interaction within these matrices would release the code inside of you and set mankind on a new and improved track. Hence your visit to Prague, etc. That the names of these matrices coincided with your own name was as coincidental as it was inevitable. The MAP is still determining if the mission succeeded, failed, or both. Desire and the socius are still being assessed. There were setbacks. *Cats* and your sudden and irrational preoccupation with ekphrasis—we foresaw these eventualities with perfect clarity. And we knew you would chase that monster to Hong Kong. But some of your actions were completely unexpected. The postcard you purchased in Deutschtown, for instance. The breakfast you ate on your sixth day in Singapore. Losing your briefcase. Brushing your teeth for an extra sixteen seconds on the evening of August 14. The dream about the yak. A lethargic rate of blinking on at least four occasions. So forth. You truly baffled us, Vincent, especially when we discovered the multivalence of your code, or rather, your unbridled selfhood. Moreover, the utter randomness of your actions was a shock to the Department of Precognition and Mythopoetic Inscription; layoffs have been rampant since the proverbial sleeper has awakened. You know how it is. Our surveillance systems are four dimensional. We perceive every citizen as a spacetime worm—the slithering pathway of your life from birth to death. But no spacetime worm is an island. There are margins of error. Glitches and aberrations invariably crop up. We can see you and we know what you've done and what you'll do...more or less. Sometimes a sound of thunder cracks open the sky and a butterfly effekt fucks everything up. What can I say? Chaos is a dirty bitch. In any event, I hope this brief exegesis has provided you with at least a modicum of comfort. Any chance you'll come back to earth and turn yourself in for decognitive estrangement? The MAP would prefer to lick this plate clean. Rest assured, your code has been extracted and projected to the far corners of existence, but one likes to be sure that there are no residual kernels in the cornhusk. Some codes are like livers: leave a piece behind after you rip the sonofobitch out and it grows right back."

Prague stopped firing the gun.

He let go of the gun and it floated away.

Cdre Rabelais nodded. "I didn't think so. Well. I suppose if we really wanted you to come home, we'd zip out there and put you in a sack. But you've been through enough. For now."

Crackle of static. Hum of turbines.

"My Ab-Crab® is dead," blurted Prague. He pulled up his shirt.

"Yes," said Rabelais.

"I'm going to let the corpse decompose inside of me." He touched the soft brown skin of his stomach.

"That's a good idea," said Rabelais.

"Eventually the sordid flakes of the apparatus will disappear into my flesh."

"Or you'll crap it out. Everything comes out in the wash."

Prague said, "Expletive."

Rabelais clutched his chest and staggered backwards. He smiled. "Do you know what your problem is? Do you, Mr Prague? You're too sane. Excessive sanity is not a handsome trait. Nor is it utilitarian. One's psyche needs to be off kilter in order to survive and excel in this world. Pull that stick of logic and causality out of your ass. You'll feel better. That's what all this is about, isn't it? You feel sad. You feel dejected and oppressed. Wildman. Nomad. You feel...*human*."

"Sir, you wanted to see me?" Another SAMSA appeared. Rabelais set him on fire with a spray can and a Zippo. A gored janitor crawled from beneath a pile of bodies and started to clean the office. Screaming, Rabelais stomped on him...

The line went dead.

Prague kicked the screen away, then closed his eyes and let himself glide down the corridor as the freighter moved closer and closer to nowhere.

# CODENAME PRAGUE

## About the Author

D. Harlan Wilson is an award-winning novelist, short story writer, literary critic, screenwriter, editor and English professor. *Codename Prague* marks the second installment of the scikungfi trilogy, the first of which is *Dr. Identity, or, Farewell to Plaquedemia*, recipient of the Wonderland Book Award in 2008. Visit Wilson online at www.dharlanwilson.com and dharlanwilson.blogspot.com.